Retreat from Murder

Retreat from Murder

Marian Babson

CHIVERS

This Large Print edition is published by Thorndike Press®, Waterville, Maine USA and by BBC Audiobooks, Ltd, Bath, England.

Published in 2005 in the U.S. by arrangement with St. Martin's Press, LLC.

Published in 2005 in the U.K. by arrangement with Constable & Robinson Ltd.

U.S. Hardcover 0-7862-7170-1 (Mystery)
U.K. Hardcover 1-4056-3232-1 (Chivers Large Print)
U.K. Softcover 1-4056-3233-X (Camden Large Print)

The text of this Large Print edition is unabridged.
Other aspects of the book may vary from the original edition.

Set in 16 pt. Plantin by Carleen Stearns.

Printed in the United States on permanent paper.

British Library Cataloguing-in-Publication Data available

Library of Congress Cataloging-in-Publication Data

Babson, Marian.
    Please do feed the cat / Marian Babson.
        p. cm.
    ISBN 0-7862-7170-1 (lg. print : hc : alk. paper)
    1. Cats — Fiction.   2. Authors — Fiction.   3. England — Fiction.   4. Cat owners — Fiction.   5. Large type books.   I. Title.
    PS3552.A25P58 2005
    813'.54—dc22   2004043137

Retreat from Murder

Chapter One

Only the long rusty blonde strands adhering to the shattered skull of the decomposing body suggested that it had once been a woman, possibly an attractive one. Now it was just a breeding ground for maggots.

'Make a tidy little profit if we could bag those things and sell them to the local fishermen for bait,' Sergeant Bullwhip quipped merrily.

'Mmm, yes . . .' Abstractedly, his companion thrust her bare hand through the squirming mass in the region of the abdomen and pulled out a gold ring; a long slimy maggot-infested string of intestine slid away as she lifted it. She shook the ring free of the remaining maggots before inspecting it.

One of the maggots struck Sergeant Bullwhip on the corner of his mouth. He recoiled instinctively, then pulled him-

self together, hawked deeply and spat. A glistening globule of green-hued sputum struck the earth just short of the corpse's outstretched fingers.

'Interesting . . .' Dr Sheherazade Wollinski observed. 'It looks as though she swallowed her wedding ring shortly before she died.' She took another look at the jawbone with some teeth unaccounted for and added, 'Either that — or someone rammed it down her throat.'

'Autopsy will tell us that, won't it?' Sergeant Bullwhip asked eagerly.

'Possibly, possibly,' Dr Sheherazade said. 'Have them remove the body to my dissecting room. It should be ready for us by midafternoon. We'll have time for lunch first.

'And, Bullwhip, bring along your smelling salts. This is going to be a juicy one . . .'

Lorinda allowed the book to slip to the floor from her nerveless grasp. Whatever had happened, she wondered, to the concept of reading as entertainment? Now it appeared to be an endurance contest as to how many pages the reader could get through before throwing up.

Had-I and But-Known moved forward

to investigate the object that had just joined the others like it on the floor. Long experience should have taught them that oblong things with fluttering pages were unlikely sources of food but, obviously, hope sprang eternal in the feline breast.

Not that she could talk. She stared ruefully at the stack of paperbacks still to be breached. It had seemed like such a good idea when she had recklessly filled her carry-on bag with what she thought was loot from the airside bookshop just before boarding her flight home. Other parcels of books from the mystery bookshops she had visited during her two-week tour of the States (plus another ten days added on as a vacation) would be arriving shortly by post. She hoped she would enjoy them more than these last-minute impulse buys. Still, she needed to keep up with what was currently popular over there.

Thankfully, however, there was no rush about it — not now that she was safely home. She leaned back and closed her eyes for a moment, savouring the peace and quiet — and the memory of that glorious moment of awakening this morning when, exhausted and disorientated, she had groped for her travelling clock with the ever-present worry: *What time do I have to check out of this hotel room?*

The clock wasn't there and she had opened her eyes to the blissful realization that she was home in her own bed. *I don't! I don't have to check out and move on! I don't have to be anywhere or do anything. I can stay in bed for the whole day if I like!* In celebration of which, she had stretched, turned over and not surfaced again for another hour and a half.

Only a year ago, she would not have believed that she could feel so happily contented in this house. At that time, Dorian King, famous mystery writer and doyen of the mystery world, had discovered the peaceful little village of Brimful Coffers and begun a determined campaign to turn it into his own fiefdom. Chivvied, perhaps slightly bullied, but definitely lured by the promise of a colony of like-minded friends and colleagues forming a retreat from the rigours of city life and its problems, a group of mystery writers had allowed themselves to be persuaded to move here.

As Dorian had painted the scene, it had sounded ideal and, as with all things that seemed too good to be true, it wasn't. During their first bleak winter, their refuge was stalked by a half-mad killer — also thoughtfully introduced into their midst by

Dorian — playing a deadly game. The killer had been caught and judged unfit to plead and was now in Broadmoor, 'detained', as the saying went, 'at the Queen's pleasure and the taxpayers' displeasure'. After which, life had gradually settled back into a more normal routine.

Perhaps Dorian was right, after all. Certainly, it had been comforting to know that the cats had been able to remain in their own home while she was away, cared for by neighbours Freddie Carlson (creator of the Wraith O'Reilly series) and Macho Magee, sweet and mild ex-history teacher, who wrote the rough-tough-Macho Magee books and was completely under the paw of his own enormous ginger cat, Roscoe.

It had been even more comforting to open the fridge door after the long taxi ride home from her red-eye flight and discover that Freddie had thoughtfully stocked it with the basics, so that she was able to have a late brunch of scrambled eggs on toast when she awoke.

Later, perhaps, she would go out and do a bit of shopping. Or perhaps she wouldn't. Freddie had provided enough so that it wasn't immediately necessary. There were also the contents of the store cupboard. A tin of soup with, perhaps, more toast would

11

do nicely for an early evening meal, followed by an early evening.

She yawned and the cats yawned back at her companionably. She ought to ring Freddie and say thank you, but she was just so tired . . .

The snick of the cat flap in the kitchen distracted her, as well as alerting Had-I and But-Known. They turned towards the doorway, waiting.

The bedraggled orange cat who staggered into the room was not immediately identifiable. It was only when Had-I and But-Known went over to him and he greeted them with a faint meow that she recognized him.

'Roscoe!' she cried. 'What's happened to you?'

Sensing sympathy and a new audience, he tottered over to her and began a long, pathetic account of his woes. Had-I and But-Known began to wash his face, one on each side of him.

'Poor darling!' Lorinda stroked his head, which seemed larger than usual and unusually bony. 'You've lost weight. Lots of it. Are you all right?' Disquiet, bordering on panic, rose in her. She must ring Macho and find out if Roscoe was ill. And whether it was anything contagious.

Had-I and But-Known began shouldering Roscoe back towards the kitchen. Lorinda stood and followed them, watching in amazement as they took him straight to their feeding bowls and seemed to be encouraging him to help himself.

He needed no urging. With a faint pathetic mewl of gratitude, he plunged in. Her cats then turned and gave her an accusing look. If she had been here, they seemed to say, this wouldn't have happened.

But what had happened? She had only arrived back late last night and had slept nearly the clock around. Still feeling the vaguely time-out-of-joint lassitude of jetlag, she had postponed getting in touch with anyone until later — much later — in the day. Perhaps it was Macho who had been taken ill and was, perforce, neglecting Roscoe.

The cats had gone back to washing their friend, offering what comfort they could along with their food. He wasn't eating quite so quickly now, but with steady determination, as though he didn't know where his next meal was coming from and so he was making sure of this one.

Lorinda started for the phone. She'd better call Freddie and find out what had been happening in her absence. She had just reached the phone when it rang.

'Welcome home!' Freddie said. 'Do you really feel you're back yet, or do you still feel half-here and half-there?'

'Half and half,' Lorinda confirmed.

'It will take a few days to get back on this time plane. It's not so bad going over, more like an extra-long day, but it's a killer coming in this direction. Time goes so skew-whiff that nothing seems quite real.'

'It's all dreamlike,' Lorinda agreed. 'I was going to ring you later, when I got a little more awake.'

'Oh, sorry. Shall I ring back?'

'No, I'm awake now. And curious. What have I missed while I've been away?'

'Now there's a question. Where to start?'

'How about with Roscoe? He popped in a few minutes ago and I almost didn't recognize him. Is he all right?'

'He's sick as a parrot,' Freddie said. 'And, if you think he's miserable, wait until you see Macho!'

'But what —'

'I'll come round,' Freddie interrupted. 'It's too much to go into over the phone. Or would you rather come here?'

'I'd rather stay right where I am, if you don't mind. I've had enough moving from

14

place to place to last me quite a while.'

'That's what I thought,' Freddie said. 'I'll be right over.'

'Oh, but I don't have anything for tea —'

'Don't worry,' Freddie said. 'I'll bring some snacks along — there's plenty for all of us. I'm awash with the stuff at the moment.'

It seemed she had hardly put the phone down when Freddie was at the door with a carrier bag full of bowls and small bulging bags. The cats raced up to their visitor eagerly.

'That's right,' she told them. 'There's more than enough for everybody.'

Roscoe headbutted her ankle enthusiastically, his purr throbbing out.

'Oh, yes?' Freddie stopped and stroked the bony head. 'Do you love me, or is it what's in the bags? Not that I'd blame you, poor baby.'

'What's the matter with him?' A faint rising panic swept over Lorinda. 'It's nothing contagious, is it?'

'No, no, nothing serious. Not to anyone else. It's pretty devastating to Roscoe, though. They've put him on a diet.'

'A diet? Macho has put Roscoe on a diet?' She couldn't believe it. 'I didn't

15

think Macho knew the meaning of the word diet.'

'Not Macho. Cressie.'

'Cressie? Who's Cressie?'

'Well you may ask.' Freddie shrugged out of her coat and tossed it across an armchair. 'You *do* have a lot of catching up to do. Cressie is living with Macho now.'

'Macho has hired a housekeeper?' She registered the amused twitch of Freddie's lips and moved on to the next obvious conclusion. 'A girlfriend? Macho has a girlfriend?'

'Of sorts. It may be more accurate to say the girlfriend has Macho. I'm not sure how happy he is with the situation, but he doesn't know how to get out of it.'

'Macho . . .' Lorinda was still stunned. 'I thought he was so traumatized by his divorce that he was never going to get involved again. How many years ago was it?'

'Yonks,' Freddie said cheerfully. 'And then he stumbles across the most unsuitable woman in the world and lets her move in with him. I'd say it serves the bloody idiot right — but nobody deserves Cressie. Especially not poor Roscoe. She doesn't know the difference between putting him on a diet and starving him to death.'

'Poor Roscoe.' Lorinda still found it hard

16

to believe, but Roscoe's scrawny state was proof of it. 'When did all this happen?'

'Just a couple of days after you left. Macho had to go up to London for an editorial conference. I gather it wasn't quite what he'd expected. He went from there to a publishing party and began drinking. Cressie was there and she'd had bad news, too, so they drank together and went on somewhere else to continue drinking when the party was over. He's a little vague about what actually happened that night, but the upshot was that she came back here with him and has been here ever since.'

'Macho? Macho got drunk? Picked up some woman? And she's living with him? Here?' It was what his character Macho Magee would have done without a second thought, but Macho's real name was Lancelot Dalrymple and it suited his own character. 'I can't imagine Lancelot Dalrymple sweeping a woman off her feet!'

'I wouldn't take any bets as to who carried whom over the threshold,' Freddie said. 'And it's not just any woman. It's Cressie Adair!'

'Cressie Adair?' Lorinda frowned. 'The name sounds faintly familiar, but . . .'

'She made a big splash a few years ago with *Hello, I'm on a Bus*. It was the cutting

17

edge of Chick Lit — and so was she. Tall, leggy, blonde — she was everywhere. You saw her picture every time you turned around. I began to think it was illegal to produce a talk show that didn't feature her. Fortunately for them, she was very opinionated. She still is.'

'Oh, yes, it's coming back to me . . . didn't she also write *Mooning the Builders*?'

'That was her second. It struck quite a chord with a lot of Upwardly Mobiles who'd bought substandard houses to renovate and were head-to-head with the cowboy builders who'd given them the lowest quote and started bumping up the charges every time they turned around. Not to mention doing a lousy job.'

'Wasn't that almost autobiographical?' Lorinda frowned again. 'I seem to remember something about accusations and threats and law suits . . . but I can't remember the outcome.'

'It all went quiet. Settled out of court, I suppose, but it was publicity for the book. And the publicity went stratospheric when she got her bum tattooed on TV with a two-fingered salute to those builders.'

'That rings a bell.'

'It should. She's used that picture of the other end of her anatomy for the author's photo on her jackets ever since. Clever of her, really . . .' Freddie nodded acknowledgement. 'She can use that picture for the rest of her life and no one can gainsay her. Quite unlike the rest of us, who have to update the old phizz every ten years or so.'

'Didn't she have a weekly column in one of the tabloids at some point?'

'Briefly, I think. The novelty of the "author's photo" at the top of the column wore off and, I gather, her opinions weren't always in line with the proprietor's. Also, her last book *Another Bloody Atrium* didn't do quite so well. Perhaps she should get another tattoo.'

'Good heavens!' Lorinda shook her head, feeling groggy. 'But, even more, I can't see her with Macho —'

'He must have really tied one on,' Freddie said. 'And so must she. Her usual prey had titles and bank accounts in seven figures. Who can explain it? It must be love. No —' Freddie broke off and shrugged. 'No, I'd say Cressie knows the meaning of a lot of obscure words — but love isn't one of them.'

Mrrrayeeeow! Roscoe registered a protest at the delay in service. He pawed at one of the bags. Something inside was driving him wild.

'What have you got in there — catnip?'

'Just food, glorious food. Poor Roscoe hasn't seen much of it lately. I fed him, of course, whenever he could get out and sneak over to me, or he'd go through your cat flap and raid Had-I and But-Known's food bowls. Only Cressie caught on to that and put him under house arrest.'

'Poor Roscoe,' Lorinda sympathized. 'You *have* been having a terrible time. But doesn't Macho intervene at all? He must see the state Roscoe is in.'

'He opens a window whenever he can get away with it, so that Roscoe can slip out and forage for himself. But, basically, Macho is the proverbial rabbit caught in the headlights as the locomotive roars towards him.'

'It sounds as though it's already hit him.'

'You're right. Perhaps I mean the man who's got a tiger by the tail.'

'The situation sounds more like the man riding a tiger, who's afraid to dismount.'

'Anyway, you've got the picture. Our Macho is helpless in the toils of a harridan. He doesn't remember how he got landed with her and he's too much of a gentleman to tell her to get out. In any case, she's got the hide of a rhinoceros and wouldn't recognize a hint if he hit her over the head with it.'

'Which, as we know, he's too much of a gentleman to do.'

'If only he could be more like his character,' Freddie sighed. 'Macho Magee would deal with her in ten seconds flat: she'd be sitting in the middle of the road with her suitcase around her neck. Also, since Macho Magee is a gentleman, too, in his own peculiar way, she'd have a one-way ticket out of town and no visible bruises.'

'No such luck with our Macho, though.'

Mrrrayeeeow! Roscoe's patience was being tried beyond endurance. He extended his claws and sank them into the plastic bag, ripping it down one side.

'All right!' Freddie swooped and pulled out a small covered bowl. 'You needn't demonstrate your bin bag technique for me. We've all seen enough of it.' She slipped off the cover and placed the bowl on the floor, stepping back hastily to get out of Roscoe's way. 'Honestly, he's turned into the local menace on rubbish collection day since Cressie's been starving him. Not a bin liner is safe from his claws. Everyone is being very understanding, but he leaves an incredible mess.'

'Poor baby.' Lorinda stooped to caress him. 'You've been having *such* a terrible time —'

'WHAT DO YOU THINK YOU'RE DOING?'

They hadn't heard the light knock at the back door and now the whirlwind was upon them. A blurred figure dashed across the room and snatched the bowl from under Roscoe's nose.

'I've told you not to feed him!' She straightened, glaring at Freddie, then transferred her fury to Lorinda. 'And that goes for you, too — whoever you are!'

'This is Lorinda. Lorinda Lucas. She lives here.' Macho had followed the woman into the kitchen. He gave Lorinda an apologetic glance. 'Welcome back.'

'And this is Cressie,' Freddie said pointedly.

'Yes, yes, I'm sorry.' Macho stood rebuked. 'This is . . . Cressie.'

'How do you do, Cressida?' Lorinda felt that a little formality was called for.

'Cressida? Cressida?' The young woman snatched back the hand she had started to proffer and looked around wildly. 'Who's Cressida?'

'Isn't that your name?' Lorinda looked to Macho, who shrugged.

'Cressida? As in *Troilus and Cressida*? That *loser*? My parents wouldn't do that to me.' She flung back her head proudly. '*My name is Crescendo!*'

'It would be,' Freddie muttered.

Roscoe took advantage of the fact that Cressie's attention was fully occupied elsewhere to steal forward and dip into the bowl that she had forgotten she was still holding.

'Stop that!' She was too late. He backed away swiftly with a long strip of chicken drooping below both jowls, giving him a Fu Manchu look.

'That cat needs better training!' Cressie snapped at Macho.

'The cat needs better feeding,' Freddie said. 'You're starving the poor thing.' She glared at Macho accusingly. 'And you're letting it happen!'

'He should have done something about the situation long ago!' Cressie, too, accused Macho. 'That damned cat was nearly too fat to walk!'

'Mmmm.' Macho gave them both a craven smile and turned to Lorinda. 'Have a nice trip?'

'Very nice.' She took pity on him and went with the change of subject. 'Tiring, though. Even with the holiday tacked on at the end, there were still lots of bits of work to do.'

'Holidays can be more exhausting than staying home and working.' Macho sounded as though he'd like to be given that choice. 'Successful, would you say?'

'Who can tell?' Lorinda sighed. 'But New York was fun — what I can remember of it — and I met some awfully nice people along the way. I only hope I'll know them if I ever see them again . . .' She thought guiltily of the small stack of business cards in her handbag. 'It's all turning into one great blur.'

'Book tours are like that,' Macho sympathized. 'At least you had a good time some of the time.'

'Book tour?' Cressie whirled on her. 'You've been on a book tour? In the States?'

'I told you —' Macho began.

'You're always telling me something!' Cressie brushed him aside, moving a step closer to Lorinda. 'How did you get an American book tour?'

'She started by having an American publisher,' Macho said, nastily for him.

'I didn't ask you!' The gold lightning bolt piercing one of Cressie's eyebrows flashed as she turned her head to glare at him. It was apparently a sore point.

'Why don't you come to dinner to-morrow night?' Freddie invited. 'She can tell you all about it then. And,' honesty seemed to compel her to admit, 'I can use you as guinea pigs for some new recipes I've found.'

'What kind of recipes?' Cressie asked, with a suspicion that spoke of previous unpleasant experience.

'Oh, I haven't decided on the menu yet,' Freddie said. 'There are so many possibilities . . .'

'I have to go up to London tomorrow,' Cressie said. 'I won't be back until late. You can go,' she told Macho ungraciously. Since when had he needed her permission?

Nevertheless, his eyes lit up, as did Freddie's. It was obviously going to be a more enjoyable evening without Cressie around.

'Would you like a —' Lorinda began.

'We can't stay,' Cressie said abruptly. 'We're expecting an important telephone call. We just came to collect the cat. Get him!' she ordered.

Macho obediently scooped Roscoe into his arms, holding him tightly. Roscoe extended his claws to hook them lightly into

Macho's jacket with a sad little *Meewrrrl.*

Clinging to each other like survivors of a shipwreck, man and cat drifted out of the house in Cressie's wake.

Chapter Two

'Whew . . .' Lorinda sank into a chair.

'You see?' So did Freddie.

'Everything except what she sees in Macho.' Lorinda frowned. 'Someone to order around, perhaps?'

'You mean a victim,' Freddie said savagely. 'Fresh blood. She's probably worn out everyone else she knows.'

'I don't see how Macho got so entangled with her. Even dead drunk, I thought he had a better sense of self-preservation than that.'

'It's a greater mystery than any we write,' Freddie agreed. 'And the greatest one of all is how we're going to get him out of this mess he's got himself into. He'll have a breakdown if that woman hangs around for much longer. Everyone is worried about him. He's lost nearly as much weight as Roscoe. I don't think she can cook at all — and, worse, she's stopped him from doing any cooking.'

'Unlike you.' Lorinda looked appreciatively at the array of dishes Freddie was now setting out on the coffee table. 'You seem to have been going mad in the kitchen.'

'Research, my dear, it's all research.'

'You're writing a cookbook?' Lorinda was bemused. Freddie was a darling and a perfectly adequate plain cook, but she was not the stuff gourmet chefs are made of.

'No such luck. I'm just trying to keep up with the latest trend. Haven't you noticed? American mysteries are full of recipes these days.'

'Not the ones I've been reading.' Lorinda glanced ruefully at the stack of waiting paperbacks. 'In fact, I'd hate to encounter a recipe in any of those. Fava beans would be the least of it!'

'Like that, is it?' Freddie assessed the pile of books. 'Well, toss 'em to me when you've done with them and I'll have a look. Shouldn't think it's my style, though.'

'It's not mine, either. I don't know what our crime world is coming to.'

'Gore galore,' Freddie sighed. 'Murder with Thai rice and Tibetan yak's cheese kebabs, drizzled with mango coulis and arsenic. Courtrooms and cats.'

'And don't forget all the ever-present serial killers. If those books were any reflection of reality, every third person you met would be a serial killer and neighbourhoods would be so depopulated they'd have to start killing each other.'

'Oh, well.' Freddie sighed again. 'Things aren't going so well anywhere. I've heard the Chick Lit boom has bottomed out. Aga Sagas are off the boil. Urban Edgy is looking over its shoulder. Things are tough in every genre and everyone is looking for the next big craze. Right now, the veering is towards children's books — but I have the uneasy feeling that they aren't as easy to do as they look.'

'I suspect you're right. I wouldn't know where to start. I don't even know any children.'

'Neither do I. Unless you want to count Rhylla's granddaughter, but I don't think she's exactly typical.'

'I should say not!' Lorinda shuddered.

'Never mind, the idea was a non-starter, anyway.' Freddie slid the clingfilm from a small plate of twig-like objects. 'Try some Cheese Whispers.'

Had-I didn't mind if she did. She thrust her head forward and neatly snapped one off the plate. But-Known was keeping her gaze firmly on a bowl of what looked like miniature meatballs and was not to be diverted by anything less.

'Very nice,' Lorinda said, surreptitiously brushing a scattering of crumbs from her skirt.

Impatient with the delay, But-Known crept closer to the bowl of meatballs and patted the clingfilm with a tentative paw.

'Keep your fur on!' Deftly, Freddie swung the bowl away from the questing paw, pulling off the clingfilm. 'And let your Mum have first go at it. You want to welcome her home properly, you know.'

But-Known wasn't too sure of that, if it meant giving up any goodies. Had-I moved over to stand beside her. Both of them watched Lorinda intently as she took a meatball and bit it in half. They transferred their attention to the remaining half.

'For heaven's sake, give them one,' Lorinda pleaded. 'I can't stand this.'

'You've weakened in your time away.' Amiably, Freddie gave each of them a meatball of their own. 'You need to get toughened up again or they'll make mincemeat of you.'

'Speaking of which, this is delicious. What is it?' Lorinda reached for another one.

'Minced lamb and rice. It's one of their favourites.'

'I'm not surprised.' They were gulping it down, one watchful eye on the bowl, determined to get more before the supply ran out.

'And it's dead easy. You don't even have to cook the rice beforehand. Just mix everything together, shape the mixture into small patties and simmer them in the soup stock until they're done, fish 'em out and serve hot or cold. We can warm these up, if you like.'

'They're fine this way.' Lorinda didn't want to face the scene that would ensue if Freddie tried to take the bowl away from the cats' anxious gaze.

'Try the chicken goujons.' Freddie uncovered another bowl.

'You've brought so much,' Lorinda protested half-heartedly. 'I don't need to eat dinner.'

'That's the whole idea. You don't want a big meal right now, your stomach's still in a different time zone. Graze — that's the answer. A nibble here, a nibble there —' Freddie blocked Had-I's lunge towards the chicken fillets, then relented and hand-fed her one. 'You, too, I suppose. Oh, yes — and you.' She repeated

31

the process with But-Known.

'Poor Roscoe . . .' Her cats' greedy enjoyment reminded Lorinda of the less fortunate. 'How he would have enjoyed all this.'

'When the situation gets desperate enough, I expect Macho will do something.' Freddie didn't sound too convinced. 'Right now, he still doesn't know what hit him. Hit them,' she corrected.

'Poor Roscoe knows something did.'

'True, but there's nothing Roscoe can do about it.' Freddie shrugged. 'And Macho is a big boy now, big enough to be in the middle of his mid-life crisis.'

'Cressie, the crisis.' Lorinda savoured the thought. 'I like it.'

'I hope Macho does. I only hope he's getting some . . . compensations . . . out of it.'

'Mmmm . . .' Stifling a yawn, Lorinda stood and crossed to the window. Perhaps a bit of fresh air would wake her up a little.

'Gemma's walking her dogs,' she observed. 'Only . . . she seems to be limping.'

'She is.' Freddie sounded uncomfortable. 'She . . . um . . . had a bit of an accident. She's a lot better now.'

'Better?' Lorinda looked after the hobbling figure and turned to face Freddie. 'What happened?'

'The pugs tripped her up. They were trying to chase a car and she couldn't control them.' Still, Freddie looked uncomfortable. 'Try some of these devilled prawns. They're very good, even if I say so myself.'

'I think it's time you said more than that.' Lorinda regarded her friend suspiciously. 'What else has been going on around here that I ought to know about? Come on,' she urged, 'you know you're going to have to tell me sooner or later.'

'I was planning to make it later,' Freddie admitted. 'You don't want to be hit with all the bad news the minute you get home.'

'How bad?'

'Bad enough. Ironic, isn't it? Although we all earn our living writing about crime, when it comes to real life, crime writers are charter members of the NIMBY and NOTE club.'

'I know NIMBY is Not In My Back Yard, but what's NOTE?'

'That's —' Freddie made a sweeping gesture — 'Not Over There, Either!'

'Gemma was mugged? Here in Brimful Coffers?' Lorinda's heart contracted as Freddie shook her head. 'Burglary, then? The dogs were trying to chase the getaway car?'

'You're halfway there,' Freddie said. 'Not burglary — but a getaway car was involved. It was a hit-and-run. One of the village children — a ten-year-old girl. The hit might have been an accident, but the run turned it into a crime.'

'Oh, no! Was the child . . . ?'

'Killed? 'Fraid so.' Freddie was distressed. 'I didn't want to tell you and spoil your homecoming, but you'd have found out as soon as you left the house and headed for the shops in the morning. You have to pass the lamp post with all the bouquets and pictures of the child tied to it. The whole corner has been turned into a sort of shrine. You can't miss it.'

'Then it happened nearby?' She thought of Rhylla's granddaughter. 'Was it anyone . . . ?'

'No one we know, thank heaven. Not that that makes it any better,' Freddie added hastily.

'That was the car the dogs chased? Then Gemma must have seen what happened. Did she get the registration number?'

'Gemma missed the whole thing.' Freddie walked over to join Lorinda at the window, looking out sadly. 'The dogs realized what was going on before she did. She just heard a dull thud and then the dogs went mad. She was trying to control them when they knocked her over and did for her ankle.'

'So she couldn't help the police at all?'

'Useless! What can you expect? Even if she'd seen the whole thing and taken notes, any evidence she gave would still be unreliable. The woman doesn't know the difference between fact and fiction.'

'She never did,' Lorinda agreed, thinking of the many manuscripts Gemma Duquesne had massacred during her reign as Fiction Editor of *Woman's Place* magazine. 'Faction was invented for — and by — people like her.'

'It was probably a stolen car, anyway. That's what it usually is in these cases. Joyriders driving too fast, teenagers and afraid to stop when they hit someone. Children killing children. It doesn't bear thinking about. I'm sorry you couldn't have come home to happier news.'

'Can't be helped.' Lorinda was horrified to discover that she was stifling another yawn. Such serious matters deserved complete attention and sympathy.

'You're exhausted.' Freddie had noticed the abortive yawn. 'Have a bit more to eat and then I'll go away and let you rest.' They turned back into the room. 'Try some of the sole goujons in lemon and dill batter. One of my better efforts, if I do say so my— Oh, no!'

Uuuurp . . . Had-I blinked and looked more embarrassed by her delicate burp than by the empty bowl in front of her. But-Known shamelessly ran a pink tongue around her chops and lowered her head for another inspection of the bowl in case there were any overlooked crumbs.

'Oh, dear!' Lorinda said guiltily. 'We should have known better than to turn our backs on them. That coffee table is too conveniently low.'

'Ah, well,' Freddie sighed. 'They're not entirely ungenerous, they've left you the cauliflower croquettes.'

'And all the dipping sauces,' Lorinda observed. 'Never mind, I did quite well up to this point. I'm not really hungry any more. Let's have another drink. No — not you!' But-Known had raised her head hopefully. 'You've had enough. You're a disgrace! Both of you!'

Unconcerned, Had-I and But-Known conferred nose-to-nose for a moment, then jumped up on to the sofa and huddled together in a corner, purring briefly before falling asleep.

This time the yawn took Lorinda unawares and was fully fledged before she could stop it. 'Oh, sorry,' she gasped.

'Don't be.' Freddie began gathering up the empty dishes. 'Have yourself an early night, sleep late in the morning and I'll see you around six thirty for dinner. Bring the cats along, too — as though you could get away from them. I can always use a couple more guinea pigs.'

'I'll look forward to it.' Lorinda followed Freddie to the door and opened it for her. 'And thank you for looking after the cats while I was away.'

But, with the capriciousness of jetlag, once Freddie had gone Lorinda found that she was no longer sleepy. Tired, yes. Ready to go to sleep, no. She pottered about the living room for a while, tidying an already tidy room, before deciding to go upstairs to bed, even though sleep didn't appear to be in view. At least she could lie down and read for a while.

She chose the book with the most innocuous cover from the lurid-jacketed pile and started up the stairs. She hadn't reached the top before discovering she was no longer alone. Even asleep, the cats were aware of her movements and were obviously determined not to let her out of their sight again. They followed her into the bedroom and leaped up on the bed to resume their interrupted nap while she went through her nightly routine and then settled herself into bed with the book.

Chapter Three

What was the saying? You have to kiss a lot of frogs before you find a prince?

And now, after all the frogs — the lager louts, the con artists, the pseuds, the useless, hopeless no-way horrors — I had found him at last. My prince: Tobias.

Darling Toby! Tall, dark, handsome, rich — and unattached.

I couldn't believe such fantastic luck. There had to be a catch — maybe twenty-two of them.

'He's probably married,' Lulu said, waving to the waiter for a fresh bottle of Chardonnay. 'With a meek little wifie hidden away in the country and three-point-six children. When number four arrives in three months' time, you'll never see him again. Because wifie has all the money, of course.' Poor Lulu based all her assumptions on her own experiences

— none of them good — with men.

'Or else he's a serial killer, preying on women with good jobs and gold credit cards.' Zizzie made up for not so much experience with a vivid imagination. 'Remember the Brides in the Bath! Remember Neville Heath! Remember —'

'He really does seem too good to be true,' quiet little Anna said apologetically.

'Leave her alone, you silly bitches! You're so jealous you can't see straight!' Desmond rose to my defence, his eyes misted with emotion. The hand not holding his glass fluttered up to press his heart. 'I think it's frightfully romantic. Good luck to her!'

'She'll need it,' Lulu muttered.

'But we'll be here for you after it all goes pear-shaped,' Zizzie said. 'What are friends for?'

I kept smiling as the Chardonnay bottle circled the table again and the last few drops fell into my glass. It was time to drop my bombshell.

'Actually,' I said casually, 'he's invited me to meet his mother tomorrow.'

'I rang the sodding RAC an hour ago! What's keeping the bastards?' Toby

kicked the front offside tyre and slammed his fist down on the bumper with such force that he hurt himself. He growled savagely, kicked the tyre again and licked his wounded hand.

'They should be along any minute now,' I soothed, telling myself that lots of men had rotten tempers when provoked. He was quite within his rights to be annoyed. 'They must have had another emergency — a crash, or something.'

'It's not good enough!' he snarled. 'We're late for tea already — and we have early dinner reservations at the Manor of the Four Winds. At this rate, it could be well after dark before we even get to Mother, let alone the Manor.'

'I'm sure they'll hold the table for us.'

'You don't understand,' he muttered. 'We're late now. Mother will be . . . horribly upset.'

'I'm sure she'll forgive you.' But his unease was infectious. She might forgive him — but would she ever forgive me?

'All right, all right.' Toby, my suave sophisticated dreamboat, was visibly unnerved and sweating. The BMW had had to be transferred to the appropriate garage and left there for major repairs.

41

Toby was not taking it well. Unless he could find alternative transport, we could forget the Manor. We might even have to spend the night at his home. I wondered how strait-laced his dear mother was. Would she allot us a double room? Or observe the conventions by giving us separate rooms, perhaps adjoining? Or express her disapproval by putting us into rooms on different floors?

The sky was darkening from a lavender twilight into the deep indigo of impending night as the RAC man dropped us at the door of the ancestral home. It took my breath away — it was practically a palace! Could I possibly live up to becoming chatelaine of such a Stately Home?

I turned to Toby, who looked even more nervous than I felt. Except for the tremor that shook his frame, he stood frozen, staring up at the great iron-bound oak door. I smiled at him reassuringly and stepped forward.

'Don't ring the bell!' He caught my hand. 'I'll use my key.' But he didn't. He hesitated, looking me up and down.

I quailed before his inspection, suddenly even more unsure of myself. Should I have worn something other than the

burgundy crushed velvet trouser suit?
Zizzie had been against it, voting for a
classic little black dress instead. Had
she been right?

But Toby wasn't looking at my cos-
tume. His gaze went to the jewellery he
had given me earlier: the ornate silver
earrings and necklace, with the match-
ing heavy solid silver cuff bracelets. He
nodded approvingly.

'Darling . . .' His voice was unsteady.
'Pay attention. This may sound strange
but . . . if you should have any trouble
with any of my family — it's unlikely
but, if you do, well — biff them on the
nose with your silver cuff bracelet!'

'Biff them . . . ? On the nose . . . ?
Toby . . .'

He inserted his key in the lock and the
door swung open. I had no option but to
follow him into the huge baronial hall.
The front door slammed shut behind us
against the encroaching blackness of the
night outside.

A welcoming fire blazed at the far end
of the great hall in a hearth not quite big
enough to roast an ox perhaps, but cer-
tainly large enough to accommodate a
suckling pig.

'Mother!' Toby called. 'We're here!'

There was a stirring beyond a doorway across the room.

'I'm terribly sorry we're so late . . . couldn't be helped. Absolute disaster with the car. Don't worry, nothing serious, only mechanical . . . but we couldn't turn back . . . I hope it's still all right . . . I mean . . .'

He was babbling. I stared at him incredulously. What had happened to my smooth intrepid hero? He was sweating more profusely than ever and his five o'clock shadow had advanced to ten o'clock. What sort of a woman was his mother to reduce him to this?

'Coming, darling,' a silvery voice called. A large Alsatian dog preceded the voice into the room.

'I couldn't help it.' Toby went on babbling. 'Complete breakdown . . . middle of nowhere . . . garage overnight at least . . . RAC dropped us here . . .'

I kept watching the shadowed doorway, waiting for the Grand Entrance. Nothing happened, although Toby still hadn't shut up. I began to get the feeling that the doorway was empty.

The Alsatian had circled me and was now advancing for full frontal confrontation, upper lip curled in a snarl — or a *sneer. There was something awfully wrong about that dog.*

Dog . . . ? Or bitch . . . ? Or . . . it looked more like a wolf . . . wolverine . . . ?

Only . . . only . . . It was wearing a pearl necklace and earrings. Its nails were lacquered a delicate pink. I felt myself swaying.

'Darling . . .' Toby was behind me, his hands steadying me . . . his elongating fingernails biting into my shoulders.

'Darling, I'd like you to meet my mother.'

Lorinda half awoke from a nightmare in which Conqueror and Lionheart, Gemma's pugs, grown to quadruple-size with elongated teeth and slavering jaws, were chasing her, Had-I and But-Known down a dark alley, heedless of Gemma's attempts to call them to heel.

The leader of their pack was now a wolverine with a gold lightning flash piercing her eyebrow and a shaved outline of a two-fingered salute on one flank. From between her vicious jaws hung the limp emaciated body of Roscoe and she was shaking it from side to side.

'What's it to you?' she howled. 'What's it to you?'

They were gaining on Lorinda. She

45

couldn't run any faster, she couldn't run any longer. She was tired . . . so tired . . .

Lorinda wrenched herself awake just before they caught her. She felt groggy and vaguely affronted. She had only spoken to Cressie for about ten minutes. How dare the woman intrude on her nightmares!

The reading light was still on, the book had fallen to the floor. The cats — Where were the cats?

She tossed back the covers and swung her feet to the floor. Almost immediately two accusing faces appeared in the doorway.

Stirring at last, are you? they seemed to say.

'What time is it?' There was a disturbing quality to the streak of daylight showing at the edge of the curtains. She wrenched them open to find her fears confirmed. The sun was definitely on the wrong side of the sky, a pale shadowy moon was becoming visible. She had slept the day away. Again.

Mrreeow! But-Known spoke briefly, but poignantly. It had been a long time since the last meal.

Yuuaaarr! Too long, Had-I agreed. They'd thought they had her better trained than that.

Guilt-stricken, as they intended, Lorinda was about to drop everything and rush to feed them when Had-I made the mistake of jumping up on the bedside table beside the clock.

'Oh, no! Is that the time?' Her guilt veered in another direction. She was overdue at Freddie's.

'You'll have to hang on a bit longer,' she told the cats as she rushed to shower and dress. 'We'll all eat at Freddie's.'

'Back for seconds, are you?' Freddie greeted the cats, then transferred her attention to Lorinda. 'You've had a good long sleep. Are you feeling better?'

'Just woke up, sorry I'm late,' Lorinda said, then Freddie's words registered. 'You mean they've been here earlier?'

'All afternoon. Supervising. After telling me a sob story about how hungry they were.'

'And you fed them. So that's why they didn't wake me! Freddie, you shouldn't let them bother you —'

'No bother. Except there'll be no giblet gravy — they got the giblets first.'

'Oh, no! You disgraceful little wretches!' Lorinda scolded.

Unconcerned, they strolled towards the

kitchen with a purposeful air.

'Macho not here yet?' Lorinda followed her hostess into the living room.

'Madam changed her mind about going to London for the afternoon, I gather, and is now going to stay overnight. He's waiting to drive her to the station.'

'That's very devoted of him; it's only a five-minute walk.'

'Devoted, nothing!' Freddie snorted. 'He wants to be sure she's well and truly gone before he smuggles Roscoe over here for a square meal.'

'Surely he manages to slip the poor creature something from his own plate once in a while? Cressie can't keep tabs on him every moment.'

'I wouldn't be too sure of that. Anyway, there's nothing to slip. I sneaked a look into his fridge when I was visiting one day and she was doing some sort of strange exercises and was safely out of the way for half an hour. There was nothing in it but three kinds of lettuce, a few other greens and a tub of cottage cheese.'

'And Macho puts up with that?' Lorinda was horrified. 'What kind of hold does she have over him?'

'I don't know, but I hope he's enjoying it. The old Macho would be out getting the barbecue ready for summer by now. Oh, I'm so glad you're back. We've tried to talk to him — but he might listen to you!'

'And he might not. If he's so besotted with that —'

The back door slammed. They exchanged glances and waited. Hesitant footsteps advanced across the kitchen floor.

'In here, Macho,' Freddie called.

'I knocked.' Macho appeared in the doorway. 'But there wasn't any answer and the door was unlocked.'

'We didn't hear you,' Freddie said cheerfully. 'Sit down and have a drink.'

'Right.' Macho lowered himself into the armchair awkwardly, trying not to disturb the sleeping cat cradled in his arms. 'Thanks.' He managed to free one hand to snatch frantically at the drink.

'Poor old Roscoe looks out for the count.' Tactfully, Freddie ignored the desperation with which Macho gulped at his drink.

'He's asleep,' Macho said unnecessarily. 'I don't know whether he's depressed or just too weak to move. He sleeps a lot now . . .' he added. 'So do I.'

'Very tiring, having a house guest,' Freddie said drily. 'Especially a long-term one.'

Macho closed his eyes, leaned back, and remained silent. Freddie shrugged at Lorinda.

Roscoe, however, was reviving. First, his whiskers twitched, then his nose, as the aroma of roasting chicken reached it. His eyes opened cautiously and he looked around, visibly relaxing to find himself among friends.

Erreow? he enquired tentatively.

In answer, Had-I and But-Known bounded in from the kitchen. He brightened still more and leaped down from Macho's lap to join them.

'*Et tu, Brutus?*' Macho asked bitterly.

'Oh, come now,' Freddie chided. 'You've brought it on yourself, you know.'

'Have I?' He regarded her bleakly. 'A lot you know about it.'

'She knows more than I do,' Lorinda said. 'Macho, what's happened? What on earth have you . . .' She faltered as he turned his baleful gaze on her.

'*Diss Me and Die!*' he snarled.

'I'm sorry.' Lorinda recoiled. 'I didn't mean to —'

'No, no,' he said. 'My new book *Diss Me and Die!* They don't want it.'

'What?'

'That editorial conference I had to go to

just after you left. It wasn't an editorial conference — it was an ambush!' The words spilled out of Macho, as though he could no longer restrain himself.

'That new editor said Macho Magee was passé. He objected to the fact that, although there were five killings in the book, not one was an evisceration. He said I'd lost the opportunity for at least three searing pages there, with each stroke of the knife being described in intimate detail.'

'Is that what they want now?' Freddie leaned back against the cushions. 'I think I feel faint.'

'He mentioned torture, too. Either before the evisceration or during it — in which the victim should be alive until the last moment, so that she could realize the full horror of what was happening to her.'

'Her?' Lorinda echoed.

'Her,' Macho said firmly. 'In fact, he complained because two of the victims were men. He said I'd lose reader sympathy that way. Everyone knew that the only proper victim these days was a beautiful blonde, leggy, busty, twenty-something who was too stupid to recognize a raving psychopath when he was drooling down her décolletage.'

'Sounds like their picture of the ideal author, too,' Freddie murmured weakly.

'I said I didn't *do* evisceration.' Macho continued his tale of woe. 'And he said that was blindingly obvious and that was why Macho Magee had fallen so far behind the times. He suggested that I go home and have a real good think about what he'd said and perhaps come back to him with a meatier story. Oh, and a lot more sex scenes.' Macho seemed on the verge of tears. 'Preferably kinky.'

'Abominable!' Lorinda sympathized, wondering whether she should pass on to him a selection of the paperbacks she had brought home. Would they help him — or just depress him further?

'So you went on from there to the launch party,' Freddie deduced. 'Or did you stop for a drink along the way?'

'What if I did?' Macho was hostile. 'What do you care?'

'I don't,' Freddie assured him. 'It's entirely understandable. So, you arrived at the party . . . and you ran into Cressie?'

'Literally. She collided with me when I was about three steps inside the door. Her drink went all over me — luckily it was white wine — and I realized her eyes were so blinded by tears that she couldn't see where she was going. I led her out into the garden where she could compose herself.'

Over his head, Lorinda and Freddie exchanged glances. Sir Lancelot to the rescue of the maiden in distress! How like Macho to pick the wrong maiden — and be stuck with her.

'Dare I ask,' Freddie ventured, 'what had upset her so?'

'It took a while before she could bring herself to tell me,' Macho admitted. 'But then we discovered we had more in common than you might think. She'd run into trouble with her latest book, too, and had had a harrowing editorial session only that afternoon. He'd told her the Chick Lit genre was becoming old hat and her new book didn't have enough *zoom* in it. Worse, he said it was understandable because she was six years older now than she was when her first book was published and, naturally, she had slipped away from the cutting edge. She hadn't introduced one new perversion in the last two books. He then mentioned that the newer, younger female writers coming along were also a lot more photogenic than she now was and he was diverting most of her former advertising budget to them.'

'No wonder she was upset,' Lorinda said.

'Devastated. It cheered her a bit when I told her about my editorial conference — and then we discovered we were talking about the same editor. We began comparing notes on him and plotting hypothetical revenge.'

'You're sure it was hypothetical?' Freddie wouldn't put anything past Cressie.

'By then, other people were coming out into the garden and the caterers were following with trays of drinks.' Macho wrinkled his forehead. 'The evening begins to get a bit blurred round about then. One drink led to another and . . . we were getting along so well . . .'

'And so you wound up back here,' Freddie said.

'Eventually . . .' Macho frowned uneasily. 'It seems to me that we went to several other places first, but I can't remember . . . Did I mention that we'd had quite a bit to drink?'

'We get the picture,' Freddie assured him.

'I wish I did.' Macho was still frowning. 'It comes back to me in bits and pieces, like a light flashing on and off in an almost empty room, where all the action is going on behind your back and you can almost-but-not-quite hear it.'

'Boy, you really tied one on!' Freddie was impressed.

'You should have seen Cressie.' Macho smiled weakly. 'One bit I do remember is that she decided we should go to that editor's home and throw rocks through his windows. I was so far gone, it seemed like a good idea to me. But, when we got there, it turned out to be a block of flats and he lived on the twelfth floor.'

'So you gave up and came home,' Freddie prompted.

'Not right away, I think.' Macho shifted uneasily. 'It seems to me that Cressie said something about another drink. It was well after hours by then, but she was a member of a private club that was open all night. I think we went there. Sort of a dark seedy district — and the club wasn't much better. Then it all goes blank again.' Macho was increasingly unhappy. 'I wish I could remember. I'm afraid . . . maybe we went to a couple of other places after that . . .' He trailed off and looked at them miserably.

'What's the matter, Macho?' Lorinda had the feeling that there was more to come — if he could bring himself to tell them.

'I wish I knew.' He turned to her apologetically. 'If only there weren't so many blanks. And, I think, right at the end, I remember Cressie grabbing my arm and shouting, "Let's get out of here!", punctuated by loud music and shouting and laughing and a lot of crashing. But I've had nightmares almost every night since then and they all end that way and I can't tell whether it really happened or I just think it did because I've heard it so often in my dreams.'

'Have you talked to Cressie about this?' Lorinda exchanged worried glances with Freddie; neither of them liked the sound of that. 'What does she say?'

'She can't remember anything, either. She wonders whether somebody put something in our drinks somewhere along the way. There are a lot of strange substances around these days.'

'And a lot of strange people.' Freddie left no doubt that, in her opinion, Cressie was one of the strangest.

'That was when we came back here . . . I think.'

'You must have taken the crack-of-dawn train.' Lorinda tried to remember when that was. '6 a.m.? 5 a.m.?'

'Earlier,' Macho said miserably. 'Too early for any train. We took a taxi.'

'*A taxi?* From *London?*' This scandalized Freddie more than anything that had gone before. 'It must have cost a fortune!'

'Where did you find a taxi at that hour?' Lorinda wondered.

'The details still escape me,' Macho admitted. 'But I seem to recall Cressie shaking me awake and demanding my wallet. I wasn't sure it had actually happened until the grandmother of all hangovers wore off a couple of days later and I discovered I didn't have a penny in the house, let alone my wallet.'

The cats had been growing increasingly restless. Now they prowled back into the room, demanding to know when they were going to be fed. Had-I and But-Known were strident and sure of themselves and their rights. Roscoe was plaintive and diffident, unsure of himself and whether his pleas would have any effect. The once-proud tom had been beaten down to a shadow of his former self psychologically as well as physically.

'Oh, poor baby!' Lorinda swept him up into her arms. He headbutted her chin gratefully, seeming to understand that he really was going to be fed properly at last.

'OOOW! Oooh!' Unbelievingly, Lorinda looked down at her own cats. One of them had just nipped her ankle.

Jealous as a cat! No wonder there was such an expression. Had-I and But-Known looked back at her with identical icy stares of umbrage and reproof. She belonged to them. How dare she make such a fuss of Roscoe? He owned a perfectly good . . . well, adequate . . . um . . . anyway . . . Macho belonged to him. And if he hadn't trained Macho correctly, it was his fault and he had no right to encroach on the sympathies of their own properly trained possession.

Arrreow! Had-I underlined.

Rrrryaah! But-Known agreed.

'That's telling her,' Freddie said. 'Now behave yourselves or you shall have no pie.'

'Children's books,' Macho said. 'Do you think . . . ? No, perhaps not . . .' He let the thought trail away, looking as dispirited as Roscoe.

'Definitely not,' Freddie said. 'Lorinda and I considered it — briefly — but decided we didn't know enough about children. Although, since you used to be a teacher, you might —'

'No,' Macho said. 'No. Better not. Cressie wouldn't like it.'

'And that would never do!' Freddie exchanged a sardonic glance with Lorinda.

You see what we're up against, she tele-pathed.

Roscoe whimpered and twisted in Lorinda's arms, as though he knew who was being discussed and it upset him.

'Food!' Freddie said firmly. 'Dinner is as ready as it will ever be. Let's eat.'

Mexican coffee cleverly replaced coffee and liqueurs by combining both. Kahlua, brandy and hot strong coffee topped by a swirl of whipped cream with just a hint of Cointreau in it, made a smooth innocuous-seeming brew. No one realized just how potentially lethal it was until Freddie had concocted a second round and they were slumped in their armchairs again, sipping it. Gradually, it seemed too much effort to do anything, least of all break up the evening and go home.

The cats were quite happy where they were. It would obviously suit Roscoe very well if he never went home — at least, not under the conditions that prevailed. Had-I and But-Known lay heavily across Lorinda's lap, pinning her down, as though, now that they had got her back, they were determined to keep her.

'Mmm . . .' Lorinda gave a contented sigh. 'Seems like old times.'

'That's right,' Freddie agreed. 'BC.'

'Perhaps not quite that long ago —' Lorinda began.

'I know what she means!' Macho lurched to his feet, suddenly belligerent, sending Roscoe tumbling to the floor. 'She's getting at Cressie again! Before Cressie! That's what she's saying!'

'Macho,' Lorinda protested. 'I'm sure she didn't mean —'

'She meant it!' Macho snarled. 'You haven't been here. She's always getting at Cressie. Well, Cressie's staying — so you'd just better get used to her! Come on, Roscoe, we're leaving — and we're not coming back until Cressie's invited, too!'

'Cressie *was* invited, but she went to London instead —' Lorinda's peacemaking was cut short by the slam of the front door.

'Damn!' Freddie said. 'I was afraid I'd mixed that coffee too strong.'

Chapter Four

Morning brought the first of the Welcome Home invitations.

'I thought just a small cocktail party Saturday,' Gemma said. 'Just our group and a few friends.'

'That would be lovely,' Lorinda said. 'But are you sure you're up to it? I've heard about your accident.'

'Oh, I'm all right. Compared to that poor child, I mean. It was such a nightmare and I feel worse because I wasn't able to be of any help at all. I've been trying and trying to remember something that might help the police, but I was watching the dogs and then I fell. I feel so useless and stupid —'

'No one could blame you,' Lorinda soothed. 'Accidents happen so quickly it's hard to sort out what actually happened.'

'Yes, well . . .' Gemma took a deep breath, obviously pulling herself together and back to the present. 'I wanted to tell you that the party is also to introduce my cousin to everyone. She's staying with me while she decides whether she wants to sublet Rhylla's flat for the summer to work on her new book. She ought to fit right in here, she's another mystery writer. She's been doing very well with her historical mysteries. Her series character is Bess of Hardwick Hall.'

'Oh, yes.' That rang a bell. 'I believe I met her in New York.'

'Oh, no, you couldn't have, dear. Opal has never been to the States. Although there's talk of her going over for the publication of her next book. You could clue her in on all the things she ought to know.'

'I'll do my best.' But did Opal really need any advice? Granted, the meeting had taken place at the beginning of her trip and she had met a lot of other people along the way, but Bess of Hardwick Hall was a distinctive enough historical figure to be memorable in herself. Oh, well, Gemma had identified the woman as a cousin. Quite probably Opal did not feel it necessary to inform every member of her family of every trip she made.

'Wonderful!' Gemma said. 'I know you'll like her. I'll look forward to seeing you on

Saturday, sixish. Although,' she added more realistically, 'I expect we'll probably run into each other around the village before then.'

'Yes,' Lorinda agreed, 'we probably will.'

Had-I and But-Known watched with interest and approval as she got out her wheeled basket and prepared to visit the shops and get in some supplies. They were unusually vocal, presumably giving her their suggestions as to what was needed.

'Yes, right,' she told them. 'You'll get what I decide we need. Although,' she conceded, 'I must say a bit of lamb's liver wouldn't go amiss.'

They agreed enthusiastically, twining around her ankles, nearly tripping her as they urged her through the door.

It was a typical late spring day, given that spring was a bit late this year. After the early heatwave she had encountered in the States, Lorinda welcomed the erratic breezes and hint of rain in the air. She stepped out briskly, noting the trees progressing from bud to tiny leaves and blossoms. She inhaled deeply, enjoying the scent of lilacs. At her feet, clusters of daffodils, tulips, roses and more exotic blooms sprinkled the grass. A cloud moved away from the sun which glowed down on the flowers, deepening their colours and making the cellophane sparkle.

Cellophane? She looked again.

Somewhere along the way, while she had been admiring the cloud formations, she had strolled into a sea of florists' blooms, still protected by their original cellophane wrappings, even though some of the flowers had withered and died.

Sparse at the fringes, the bouquets thickened into a solid carpet surrounding a lamp post. More bouquets were tied to the lamp post, as were several miniature teddy bears and a selection of small soft toys. Surmounting it all was a photograph of a little girl, smiling trustingly out into a world she would never see again.

This must have been where it had happened. Farther on, at a respectful distance from the shrine, stood the yellow sign headed 'ACCIDENT' in large black letters, while smaller letters spelled out the police appeal for information from anyone who might have witnessed the accident.

It was as well Freddie had warned her about this: it was no sight to stumble on unprepared.

Moving closer, she could read the sad little notes from school friends and family pinned to the various bouquets. Such a brutal waste of life, such a shock for her schoolmates, such devastation for her parents.

Lorinda moved slowly on her way, feeling guilty because of the relief she also felt. Freddie was right: it was no one they knew.

'A terrible thing.' The voice spoke from behind her. 'Just terrible.' Betty Alvin, Dorian's part-time secretary and occasional typist for others in the group, quickened her pace to fall into step beside her. 'Everyone is shocked. One doesn't expect that sort of thing in a place like this.'

'Mmm,' Lorinda murmured non-committally. After the spate of murders that had occurred in their midst last year, she would have thought that that was just the sort of thing that people would expect.

'Gemma, especially,' Betty prattled on. 'To think that she was an eyewitness and she let those dogs distract her so much that she didn't see a thing!'

'That ankle must have been quite painful, too,' Lorinda said. 'No wonder she couldn't pay attention to everything that was happening.'

'Oh.' Betty was disappointed. 'You've heard.'

'I've talked to Gemma.' It seemed kinder

to let Betty believe that she had had a first-hand report, rather than a briefing from Freddie first. To further cheer Betty (after all, there was a sort of diary of her trip to be typed eventually), she asked, 'How's Dorian?'

'So-so.' Betty cheered up immediately. 'But not so bad as he's pretending, I think. Do you know —' she lowered her voice — 'he's still using a walking stick — and I'm sure he doesn't really need it any more.'

'No!' Lorinda reacted obligingly with the expected shock, but wasn't at all surprised. Typical of Dorian. He'd never let go of a good pose until he'd milked it for all it was worth.

'And you wouldn't believe the letters he's written to the insurance company!'

Oh, yes, she would.

'He's trying to make it sound as though he's been crippled for life. It would serve him right if they sent someone round to check on him.'

'He *was* very badly hurt.' Lorinda would never forget seeing his body sprawled across the desk, blood oozing into the old-fashioned green blotter. 'I wasn't sure he'd survive.'

'Hmmph!' Betty sniffed. 'You needn't worry about him. He'll outlive us all!'

'Quite likely,' Lorinda agreed absently. They had reached the greengrocer's and she began mentally debating the merits of imported cherry tomatoes versus home-grown early-crop Lancashire peas, although she knew she would undoubtedly wind up buying them both, plus Jersey Royal new potatoes and . . .

'Well, I'll leave you to get on with your errands.' Betty recognized that she had lost her audience for the time being and crossed the street to the post office, pointedly looking carefully in both directions before she stepped off the kerb.

Macho was already at the counter being waited on when Lorinda arrived at the butcher's. He gave her a guilty nod. 'And half a pound of sausages,' he said in an undertone to the butcher, glancing over his shoulder to make sure that no one else had entered the shop.

'That the lot?' The butcher swirled an outer covering of striped paper around the order and placed it atop a pile of similarly wrapped packages. At Macho's nod of agreement, he shook open a plastic carrier bag and began loading the purchases into it, naming a total that raised Lorinda's eyebrows.

'And what would you like?' The butcher

took Macho's money and transferred his attention to Lorinda. 'Nice to see you back. Have a good trip?'

'Lovely, thanks. A pound of lamb's liver, half a pound of streaky bacon and, I think, a couple of —'

'What are you doing in here?' an icy voice demanded from the doorway. 'And what have you got there?' Cressie advanced on Macho, glaring at the carrier bag he had just acquired.

'Hers! . . . It's h-h-hers,' Macho stammered, pointing to Lorinda. 'I'm just c-c-carrying it for her.'

'She's got a shopping cart! What's wrong with that?'

'I — I — don't know.' Macho looked to Lorinda beseechingly, but she couldn't claim that her cart was full. Cressie was quite capable of lifting the lid and proving her a liar. 'I — I — didn't think.'

The butcher turned away, his shoulders quaking suspiciously. Lorinda got the impression that he had seen Cressie in action before. When he turned back, he caught her own eye meaningfully and held out her parcel tentatively.

'Is that yours, too?' Cressie didn't miss a thing. 'Aren't you buying rather a lot — for one person?'

'I'm restocking my freezer,' Lorinda replied smoothly. 'If that's quite all right with you?' She could be rude, too.

'I'll put it on your bill, shall I, love?' The butcher cleverly avoided the subject of payment. Cressie would have noticed that the price asked was too small for the amount of shopping.

'Thank you.' Lorinda deposited the small parcel in her basket and Macho hurriedly flung his carrier bag in on top of it.

'Honestly, you don't know what I have to put up with!' Cressie's complaint was obviously as close to an apology as she was able to get. 'He's always trying to sneak food to that overstuffed monster of his. It was a good thing I saw him from the taxi as he was going in here.'

'You took another taxi from London?' Macho asked.

'No, from the station. Well, I couldn't walk it with two heavy suitcases, could I?'

'Suitcases?' Macho paled.

'I do need a change of clothes occasionally. And I wanted some manuscripts I've been working on.'

'Oh, yes . . . yes, of course . . .' Macho's attention had drifted back to the counter where the butcher was feeding off-cuts of lamb into a hopper and long delicious-

69

looking strands of mince were emerging from the grinder. Lamb burgers had always been one of his barbecue specialities.

'Come along,' Cressie said briskly. 'There's nothing for us here. I've picked up a couple of ready-meals in town. Macaroni cheese, and spinach and ricotta cannelloni — you can take your pick.'

'Oh . . . fine.' Macho did not even bother with a pretence of enthusiasm.

'I still have to get to the bakery.' Lorinda could stand the piteous sight no longer. 'I'll see you at Gemma's party.'

'Yes.' He brightened. 'Yes, it's your welcome home. It's so good to have you back.'

'Yeah.' Cressie's narrowed eyes swivelled between Macho and Lorinda's shopping basket with dark suspicion. 'Just great.' She saw to it that they preceded Lorinda out of the shop and frowned when Macho paused to hold the door open for Lorinda.

Lorinda hoped that Cressie did not notice Roscoe skulking behind a neighbouring waste bin and a couple of bin bags. His baleful gaze followed Macho and Cressie as they turned towards home. Then he turned on the nearest bin bag and, with a savage sweep of his claws, ripped it apart. Somehow, he left no doubt as to just whose flesh he wished it was.

And Roscoe had always been such a gentle, sweet-natured cat. What had that woman done to him? What had she done to Macho?

Chapter Five

'You might have told me you were going to the States.' Dorian King sounded distinctly pettish. 'I could have given you any number of people to look up. They'd have shown you a wonderful time.'

'I *had* a wonderful time.' Lorinda took a deep breath and tried not to sound pettish herself. 'It all happened very suddenly when there was what they called "a window of opportunity". Besides,' she remembered, 'you weren't around. You were away on one of your cruises.'

'You needn't say it as though I were off on some sort of jaunt. It was a necessary part of my convalescence. I was nearly murdered, you know.'

' "Nearly" doesn't count.' Freddie had come up behind them.

'I'm surprised you don't say "Better luck next time." ' Yes, he was in a very waspish mood. Perhaps he had a right to be. His injuries had been quite fearsome, even considering that head wounds were notoriously bloody. Yet there seemed to be an extra edginess in the way he looked around the party. The killer had been caught and was awaiting trial. Surely, Dorian couldn't still be in fear of his life. He was safe among friends now.

'I might say that yet,' Freddie assured him. 'What's this rumour I've been hearing about you?'

'Which rumour is that?' Dorian's tone was guarded; judging from his expression there could be a wide choice of rumours.

'The one about your . . . impending house guest. Your . . . protégée.'

'Nothing of the sort,' he denied quickly. 'A mere colleague, an acquaintance from New York. She's coming over to do research for her historical series. Naturally, I invited her to stay with me, since I have so much room.'

'Historicals seem to be flying high these days,' Freddie observed. 'Have you met Gemma's cousin yet? She'd be a good one to get together with your house guest. They ought to have a lot in common.'

Lorinda blinked. Was it her imagination, or had Dorian suddenly gone several shades paler? Was he all right?

'Er, yes,' he said uneasily. 'Yes, no doubt.' He looked across the lobby to the makeshift bar where Gemma and her Cousin Opal were holding forth.

'Why don't we sit down?' Lorinda suggested, adding hastily, as Dorian's mouth tightened, 'I'm afraid I'm still feeling a bit jetlagged and dizzy.'

'Oh, very well.' Since it was her weakness, he could pander to it. They settled themselves on the padded top of a window seat nestled between the marble arches framing the comfortable niche. The silver handle of Dorian's ebony walking stick glittered as he raised it in an imperious gesture.

Betty Alvin immediately headed in their direction, detouring only to catch up a tray of canapés from a nearby table.

'Ah, excellent.' That was obviously what Dorian had wanted. 'And, while you're about it, why don't you commandeer a bottle of that Chardonnay and freshen our drinks?'

'Yes, of course.' Betty nodded and obediently trotted off towards the table where the bottles were arrayed.

'Really, Dorian, you're impossible!' Freddy said. 'Betty is not only off duty, she's a guest, like the rest of us. She shouldn't be running your errands.'

'She doesn't mind.' Dorian sounded mildly surprised at the reprimand. 'She's very —' He leaned against a marble arch and his eyes widened in amazement.

'. . . *pack of self-satisfied, middle-class, middle-aged, mid-list second-raters . . .*' The others could hear the woman's voice now, low and venomous, as she ranted on. '. . . *never seen a mean street, or a corpse in their lives . . . nerve to write about it . . .*'

'Well!' Dorian had regained his breath, his eyes narrowed. 'Nice to know what people think of us.'

' "Would some power the giftie give us",' Freddie quoted.

'This place is a whispering gallery,' Lorinda explained. 'We discovered that a while ago. It's all the marble, I suppose —'

'. . . *my friends . . .*' They hadn't needed to hear Macho's voice to know who must have been speaking. '. . . *and, I can assure you, we've all seen our share of — murder victims — in the past few months.*'

'I'll never know what he sees in her,' Freddie complained. 'You'd think —'

'. . . *chance to break out . . . can't weaken now . . . you've got to . . .*' The voice died away and they looked across the room to see Cressie and Macho emerge from one of the alcoves opposite them.

'What does she want him to do?' Freddie wondered what they were all wondering. Nothing he really wanted to do, judging from the expression on Macho's face.

'Here we are!' Gemma rushed up to them, flourishing a bottle. 'Betty said you were running low. Can't have that!' She poured briskly.

Betty Alvin, Lorinda saw, had just been cornered by Cressie and was not looking any happier than Macho as Cressie harangued them both.

The few local shopkeepers Gemma had invited were clustered together, except for Jennifer Lane of the bookshop, who was talking to — or rather, listening to — Cousin Opal. From the look on her face, she was finding Opal a bit wearing.

'It's going rather well, I think.' Gemma looked around and gave a satisfied nod. 'Everyone is here except Hilda Saint — she warned me she might be late. She's having an extension built on her guest house and she tries to supervise the builders as much as possible to make sure they keep working — they seem to be an awkward lot.'

'Aren't they always?' She might be awkward, too, Lorinda thought, if she had to have Hilda Saint constantly hovering to make sure she was getting her money's worth.

'Oh, and I have a message for you from Professor Borley.' Gemma gave Lorinda an arch look. 'Such a charming man! He's at some conference in Oxford this week, but he's delighted that you're back and is looking forward to being able to interview you soon.'

'Thanks,' Lorinda said bleakly. She supposed it had been too much to hope that the American academic had forgotten about the interview he wanted. She liked the professor well enough, but would have liked him better had he not decided that his next entry in the academic Publish or Perish Stakes was going to be an in-depth study of English mystery writers in their native habitat: Brimful Coffers.

'Isn't his sabbatical year just about up?' Freddie felt the same. 'He seems to have been hanging about here for ever.'

'Oh, I believe he still has another month or so in hand. And,' Gemma added enthusiastically, 'he says he might be able to get a bit of an extension if his work is going well.'

'Mmmm.' Freddie was not so enthusiastic.

'So you needn't worry,' Gemma went on.

'Our happy little group isn't going to be broken up yet. In fact —' she gave Dorian another of her arch looks — 'I gather more happy reunions are in the offing. I hear you've had a postcard from Edinburgh . . . ?' She waited expectantly.

'Ermm . . . yes.' After a long pause, Dorian decided to respond. 'The Jackleys are back from the Continent and doing some touring around Britain at the moment. They say they're looking forward to being back in Brimful Coffers soon.'

'That's a blow.' Freddie was not pleased at the news that her neighbours in the other half of her semi-detached were returning. 'I was hoping they'd succeeded in killing each other by now.'

Dorian gave an involuntary nod of agreement which he tried to disguise by a sudden coughing fit. Obviously, the thought of Karla Jackley back in pursuit of him was no more welcome than Lorinda's threatened interview.

'Oh, it will be nice to have us all back together again,' Gemma gushed. 'It will be so healing — after all we went through. If only . . .' Her face darkened. 'That poor child . . .'

'You're brooding about it again!' Her Cousin Opal swept up to them, Jennifer

Lane trailing reluctantly in her wake. 'I can tell by the expression on your face. You've got to stop! It wasn't your fault! You weren't driving the car!'

'I know, I know,' Gemma wailed. 'But I can't help feeling that I should have been able to do more. I couldn't even tell the police what kind of car it was. And I must have seen something that would give them a clue!'

Her words rang out into one of those abrupt silences that can fall over a group. There was a theory, wasn't there, Lorinda seemed to recall, that these fell at twenty minutes to, or twenty minutes past, the hour. She was surreptitiously glancing at her watch to check the time when Gemma's voice rang out again.

'I feel so awful about it that . . .' Gemma lowered her voice and leaned closer to them. 'That I'm thinking of volunteering to be hypnotized! They say you can re-member all sorts of things you think you never noticed at the time if a professional hypnotist regresses you.'

'It's worth considering.' Her cousin nodded. 'It might even work. You'd have nothing to lose.'

'Exactly. And it might make her family feel better. At least, then, they'd know we'd tried everything.'

'Sorry about the delay.' Betty Alvin, having broken free of Cressie, bustled up to them with a bottle. 'Oh — you've already been topped up.'

'Don't go away.' Dorian was looking a bit frayed. 'It won't be long before we can use another.'

'So kind of you to help, dear,' Gemma said, automatically scanning the room to make certain all her guests were happy. A faint frown rumpled her forehead as her gaze rested on Macho, then moved away. There was nothing even the most perfect of hostesses could do to rescue him from his predicament.

'I can't stay much longer,' Dorian said abruptly. 'I'm expecting a call from my agent. Something about a lecture tour. I suppose I shall have to do it.' He did not look as reluctant as his words suggested.

'What a shame,' Gemma sympathized. 'They're working you too hard.'

A muffled snort from Betty Alvin reminded the others who did most of the hard work. Gemma didn't notice the hidden message but, unfortunately, brought her attention to bear on the communal secretary.

'Opal, have you had a chance to discuss

things with Betty yet? I know your dead-line is coming up and —'

'No!' Betty's voice rose. 'No, I'm sorry. I can't do it! She's not the only one with a deadline. I can't take on any more work!'

Lorinda and Freddie shifted guiltily. Per-haps, Lorinda decided, she wouldn't ask Betty to type up the diary she'd been keeping on her trip — at least, not yet.

'Oh, but surely —' Gemma, made of sterner stuff, was not so easily discour-aged.

'No!' Betty slammed the bottle down on the table. The bottle swayed, but did not break. The same could not be said for Betty.

'I can't *do* all this! There's only one of me — and there's more of you every day! Even that tart of Macho's thinks I have nothing better to do than drop everything whenever she waves a manuscript in my di-rection!' Her voice was higher, she was perilously close to tears or hysteria — or both. 'I can't! I can't! I can't!' She whirled and rushed for the back stairs leading up to her attic quarters.

'Well!' Gemma said to Opal. 'We'll just have to wait and talk to her when she's in a better mood.'

'It's not like Betty to throw a wobbly like

that.' Dorian frowned. 'Have you all been pushing her too hard? I have first call on her services, remember, and I'll want my lecture notes sorted out and the first draft of the new book ready to take with me to work on while I'm touring.'

Poor Betty. How she must rue the day she allowed Dorian to talk her into taking up residence in Brimful Coffers. It was fortunate that Dorian hadn't decided to move her into the housekeeper's rooms in the Manor House. Of course, that would have cramped his style with the various ladies who floated into and out of his life. Which might have been the reason he hadn't yet acquired a housekeeper and depended on the services of a daytime cook and cleaner from the village.

'Has something upset Betty?' Macho sidled up, looking as guilty as Lorinda felt. Cressie strode behind him.

'I don't know why you rave about that woman.' Cressie sent a contemptuous glance at Betty's retreating back. 'She isn't at all helpful. In fact, she's the most obstructive person I've ever met.'

'She helps *us*.' Freddie sent Cressie a glance of her own. Cressie was undoubtedly an expert on obstructive people. The way she talked to them was not likely to bring out their co-operative qualities.

'We've never had any problem with her.' Lorinda backed Freddie.

'Well, I don't know how you do it.'

'Perhaps it's because we say please.' Freddie darted a look at Dorian. 'Most of us.'

'But I offered her double pay.' Cressie was uncomprehending.

'Really?' Gemma's eyebrows arched meaningfully at Opal. 'That's hardly fair play. No wonder Betty is so upset. It isn't done to bribe your way to the front of the queue. Betty takes everyone in turn as they come along.'

'Macho was in the queue already.' Cressie gave her a poisonous look. 'Just because he's changed his mind about what he's going to write, she wants to treat it as a new assignment. That's not fair!'

'Oh, look!' Gemma was not prepared to debate the subject any longer. 'There's Hilda now!' She waved to the guest house proprietor, who had just arrived. Hilda waved back feebly and moved towards the drinks table.

'Oh, dear, she *does* look frazzled! I must talk to her . . .' Expertly, Gemma slid away from the group and headed for the new arrival, Opal following in her wake.

The others turned their attention to Macho, who quailed at the flurry of interest generated by Cressie's revelation. Not that some of them hadn't suspected it already, but it was satisfying to have their deductions confirmed. They waited to see whether further information would be forthcoming.

Not from Macho; he retreated behind Cressie, kicking her sharply on the ankle as he passed.

'Right, right, I remember. I was just saying —'

'Well, don't!' he snapped.

This time he got the poisonous glare. Cressie picked up a truncated celery stalk and swirled it in the bowl of houmous.

'Not even taramasalata!' Macho found another source of complaint as he surveyed the vegetarian spread provided with the drinks. A large platter of crudities was flanked by bowls of houmous, dal, green olive tapenade and the inevitable onion-and-sour-cream dip. Other bowls contained marinaded mushrooms, black olives glistening with oil and speckled with herbs, green olives stuffed with pimentos or anchovies, cheese straws and mixed nuts.

All very healthy and tasty, but nothing to bring home to a hopeful cat.

'Gemma's not so dumb,' Freddie observed. 'She doesn't intend to feed all the neighbourhood pets.'

'Considering the amount she snaffles for her own brutes at every party, it isn't very sporting of her,' Macho grumbled.

'I never said she was sporting.' Freddie nodded at Gemma's retreating form. 'Just smart. In her way.'

'Which is not our way.' Dorian gazed speculatively at the departing backs. 'What do you think of that cousin of hers? Does she look like a troublemaker to you?'

'What do troublemakers look like?' Freddie wondered.

'She hasn't really said enough for us to formulate any opinion of her,' Lorinda temporized.

'Why is he worried about troublemakers?' Macho muttered. 'Is he afraid of competition?'

Cressie took another piece of celery and crunched it loudly.

Abruptly, Lorinda longed to go back home and settle down with a good book — or any book on which someone else had done all the work.

Chapter Six

'Mmmff, ooaah, umph,' *he moaned.*

'You'll have to speak up,' I told him. 'I can't understand a word you're saying.'

'Mmfff, oooah, ummph.' He tried again, rolling his eyes desperately and twitching.

It was his own fault. He'd insisted on the thumbscrew being applied to his tongue. I'd heard him myself. What else could Delilah do but oblige? He was the paying customer.

'He's doing it on purpose,' Murgatroyd gurgled from the floor at my feet. 'Hit him! Kick him in the balls! Show him who's boss!'

'I can't kick him,' I said. 'I'm not wearing my stiletto heels.'

'Use the cigarette lighter!' Murgatroyd rolled over and licked my toes.

'Will you two kindly shut up?' I moved my feet away. 'I'm trying to watch television.'

'Mmmfff! Mmmfff!' *Mr Smith fell to his knees and began banging his head on the arm of the couch.*

Maybe I should do something, he was beginning to turn blue. But I hated to interfere with Delilah's business.

'At least throw your drink in his face,' Murgatroyd *said,* 'or he'll think you don't love him.'

'I don't,' *I said.* 'I don't even like him — or you. I think you're absolutely disgusting!'

'Oh, that hurt!' Murgatroyd *gasped.* 'That really hurt! Thank you.'

Mr Smith had fallen strangely silent. I looked at him uneasily. Delilah had the key to his handcuffs. I knew she was busy with a special customer, but I wondered if I could knock on the door and disturb her for just a minute. I wasn't used to this and Smith was making me nervous.

'Stop!' Murgatroyd *hurled himself in front of me, trying to trip me as I started towards the Inner Sanctum.* 'You can't interrupt her. It's against the rules.'

'You have rules?' *It was news to me.* 'Well, they're nothing to do with me. I can't —'

'OHGODOHGODohgodohgod!'   *The*

87

door opened abruptly and Delilah hurtled through it. 'He's snuffed it! I just left him tied up in the closet with the ferret and the baby boa constrictor for a couple of hours and I come back and he's snuffed! Do something!'

'For God's sake, Delilah! That's the second corpse this month and it's only the thirteenth. You've got to stop throwing yourself into your work this way!'

'Friday the thirteenth,' Murgatroyd giggled. 'Unlucky for some . . .'

'I didn't do it!' she wailed. 'I didn't do the other one, either! We've got to get him out of here! If the landlord finds out, he'll break my lease!'

'We'll help you,' Murgatroyd said eagerly. 'We did the last time, remember? Just untie us and we'll carry him out.'

Smith, who seemed to have revived, nodded eagerly. As a Captain of Industry, he blossomed at the prospect of action.

'Oh, would you?' Delilah flew over to Smith and removed the thumbscrew from his tongue. 'I'd be ever so grateful.' To prove it, she twisted the instrument as she pulled it free and he reeled. 'Ever so.'

It just goes to show: you never know

how your old school friends are going to end up. It had seemed like such a good idea when Delilah wrote offering me a room in her flat for a very nominal rent if I wanted to move to the city. How was I to know the career path she had decided to follow?

I just knew one thing for certain. Once I had enough money to get out of here, I was never again going to share a flat with a Dominatrix.

And this had been described on the cover as 'a delightful introduction to a sparkling new genre: Cosy Noir'!

Lorinda hurled the book into the growing heap at the far corner of the room, glad that she had waited until morning before trying to settle down with it.

At least she had the rest of the day free now to do something else. If only she could decide what she really wanted to do. She was not yet in the mood to get on with the books in progress. The backlog of housework definitely did not appeal.

She prowled restlessly over to the window, in time to see a taxi sweep past and take the turning that led up to the Manor House. Presumably, Dorian's guest arriving. That meant another welcoming cocktail party was on the cards.

A moment later, Gemma and her cousin hove into view, each holding a leash for one of the pugs. Lorinda looked after them wistfully. A walk would be nice, especially with a dog or two to add purpose to it. Lovely as they were, cats weren't quite the same.

Thinking of which, where were Had-I and But-Known? She hadn't seen them for some time. Either they hadn't quite forgiven her desertion of them, or Freddie was cooking again. She crossed to the telephone.

'Do you have my lot cluttering up your kitchen?' she asked when Freddie answered.

'Are you referring to my Tasting Panel?' Freddie replied. 'I'm afraid they're working and can't be disturbed right now. They're sitting in front of the oven, willing it to cook faster. Come over and join them, the latest experiment is just about ready to serve.'

The cats barely turned their heads when Freddie opened the back door to let her in. They did, indeed, appear to be exerting every ounce of willpower to urge the cooker to complete its task.

'Sorry to barge in on you again,' Lorinda

apologized, 'but I just can't seem to settle.'

'It *is* difficult,' Freddie commiserated. 'It always takes me ages when I get back from a trip.'

'I know.' Lorinda settled down at the table and sniffed the fragrant air as appreciatively as the cats. 'But I always hope it won't take so long this time.'

'You're such an optimist.' Freddie poured coffee. 'Start on that and the mini-muffins will be ready to come out of the oven before our second cup.'

'Wonderful.' Lorinda sipped the hot delicious brew and felt the restless formless anxiety that had plagued her begin to subside. There was no train or plane she had to catch, no signing where she had to preside and be gracious, no worries about missing buttons or lipstick on her teeth. She was home, safe and secure among friends. Nothing could bother her now —

'Freddie!' The back door burst open and slammed against the wall. The cats jumped and turned to stare accusingly at the noisy intruder.

'Freddie!' Macho staggered into the room. 'Lorinda!' He reached the table and grasped its edge desperately, swaying and trying to stay upright.

'Macho, what is it?' Alarmed, both

women jumped to their feet, ignoring the coffee splashing into their saucers and spilling on to the table.

'Help!' he croaked. 'Help!' He gave a wild laugh. 'But there is no help!'

'Macho!' Lorinda gripped his heaving shoulders, unsure of whether to shake him or cradle him. 'What's wrong?'

'Cressie!' he gasped. 'Cressie!'

'Oh.' Freddie looked at Lorinda. They might have guessed.

'No! No, you don't understand!' He caught Freddie's wrist, not noticing her wince of pain. 'Cressie — she's dead!'

'Don't worry,' Freddie said. 'No jury on earth would convict you.'

'No! No!' Macho cried. 'I didn't do it! I never laid a finger on her!'

'Are you sure?' Lorinda asked. 'That she's dead, I mean,' she added hastily.

'I found her! I've just got back from shopping and —' Macho snatched up the nearest cup of coffee and drained what was left of it. 'I opened the front door and found her! Lying at the foot of the stairs! Covered in blood!' He finished the other cup of coffee and stared around wildly.

The cats looked at him, then at each other and, moving as one, retreated to a far corner of the room. Lucky cats, Lorinda thought, the humans didn't have that option.

'Let's get over there!' Freddie moved forward, Lorinda right behind her.

'But what about the police . . .' Macho held back. 'An ambulance . . .' He shuddered. 'This can't be happening again.'

'Come on.' Lorinda linked arms with him and urged him along. 'It may not be as bad as you think. Let's go and see.'

'No, please . . .' Macho was protesting all the way. 'Not the front door. I can't walk in on that scene again. Use the back door.'

'We will,' Lorinda soothed, wondering why he thought the scene might improve if viewed from a different angle. She fought against a mounting surge of irritation. Even dead, Cressie was a nuisance. Especially dead.

As they entered the front hallway from the kitchen, they saw the shopping bag Macho had dropped just inside the front door. Several packages spilled from it, two of them wrapped in the distinctive striped paper the butcher used. A telltale blob of red saturated a corner of one of them. Blood leaking from the meat, or from . . . ?

As they moved forward, she could see a shoe lying on its side. One of the large clumpy shoes currently in fashion which looked as though they were a danger to any wearer with the slightest tendency to clumsiness. Running up or down a flight of stairs in those . . .

Now they could see the foot and, crouching midway between it and the shopping bag, Roscoe, staring intently from one to the other. Hungry as he constantly was these days, he was showing unusual restraint in not attacking one of the butcher's packages. Even dead, Cressie seemed to have traumatized both Roscoe and his master so thoroughly that they were unable to function normally.

'Here, boy.' Keeping his face averted from the staircase, Macho went forward and picked up Roscoe. 'It's all right, boy. It's all right.'

It patently wasn't. While Macho did not want to look at Cressie's body, Roscoe could not stop staring at it. The tip of his tail twitched slowly and rhythmically. He might have been watching at a mousehole.

Lorinda found herself on Macho's side. She did not want to look, either.

Freddie was more intrepid. Moving slowly and carefully, she circled the body and stood looking down. Lorinda forced herself to go over and stand beside her.

There was an awful lot of blood. Dried

blood. Smeared over Cressie's face and neck, arms and hands, the dark reddish-brown coagulating blood was a gruesome sight, not to be looked at too closely. An arteryful of blood. But . . . didn't arteries spurt? And . . . where was the break in the skin from which all that blood could escape?

'How long were you out shopping, Macho?' Freddie asked.

'About an hour.' Macho still would not look in their direction. He cradled Roscoe and added defensively, 'She was perfectly all right when I left.'

'Freddie . . . ?' Lorinda had a question of her own. 'How long does it take blood to dry?'

'Good question.' Freddie bent closer to the inert form and took several deep sniffs before straightening up with a triumphant look.

'Up, Cressie!' She prodded Cressie's ribs with a none-too-gentle toe. 'Up! The game is over. You've been rumbled!'

In the long moment that followed, Macho and Lorinda drew closer. Lorinda did some sniffing of her own with a dawning suspicion . . . there was something awfully familiar about the scent reaching her nostrils.

'What do you mean?' Macho looked from Cressie, who had not moved, to Freddie, who was drawing back her foot again. 'No, don't kick her! She's —'

'She's shamming — and you're the one who ought to kick her! That isn't blood — that's Angostura bitters!'

'Of course!' The vaguely familiar scent identified, Lorinda could not imagine why she had not recognized it at once. On the occasions when drops had flown astray in the cocktail mixing process, she had even noticed the resemblance to blood herself.

'Gotcha!' Cressie's braying laugh rang out as she rolled away before Freddie's foot reached her again. 'Told you none of you would recognize a dead body if you saw one. Now I've proved it! You fell for it! All of you!'

'Not for long,' Freddie said grimly.

'Long enough!' She was triumphant. 'Long enough to send him —' she gestured dismissively towards Macho — 'running like a frightened rabbit! Or maybe I should say a scaredy-cat. Yeah, that's right — scaredy-cat! Even the cat was braver than you. At least it came close enough to sniff!'

And that was why Roscoe had resisted the pull of the butcher's parcels. He had known she wouldn't let him get away with it. Whatever games she might be playing, she was still an active and dangerous force.

'You're disgusting!' Macho's colour had been returning to normal, now he paled again.

'Macho is right. Go and wash your face!' If Cressie wanted to act like a child, Freddie was prepared to treat her as one. 'And change your clothes. Although,' Freddie added with gleeful malice, 'I wouldn't be prepared to bet you'll ever get those stains out. I hope you weren't planning on ever wearing that outfit again.'

'Oh!' Obviously, Cressie had not thought of that. She squinted down at her ruined top, although most of the damage was around the neckline and not visible to her. For a moment, she looked childlike and vulnerable.

'I don't care!' Abruptly, she shrugged herself back into her normal persona. 'I can buy more. Plenty more!' She whirled away, snatched up her shoe and dashed up the stairs. A door slammed defiantly.

'Macho . . .' Lorinda began tentatively.

'That woman is poison!' Freddie was not prepared to be discreet. 'You've got to get rid of her!'

'I can't.' Macho would not meet their eyes. Roscoe gave a protesting squeal as

Macho clutched him tighter. 'Don't you see? I can't!'

He turned unseeingly and blundered into his study. The door slammed behind him, too.

Chapter Seven

A strong smell of burning greeted them as they opened the back door into Freddie's kitchen. Had-I and But-Known trotted forward, uttering loud complaints and recriminations.

'Oh, no — the muffins!' Freddie caught up a pot-holder and swung the oven door open. A dark cloud eddied out and swirled around the kitchen, setting them coughing.

'Ruined . . .' Freddie mourned, backing away from the smoke and bending down for a better look. 'They're not actually alight, though.'

'You'd better let everything cool down a bit,' Lorinda warned as Freddie reached for the pan. 'And find another pot-holder — you're going to need both hands.'

Had-I added an observation of her own, which might have been helpful if translatable.

'There are no two ways about it . . .'

Freddie abandoned the oven and turned to brewing a fresh pot of coffee. 'No matter what Macho says, that woman has got to go!'

'Well, you heard him. He couldn't have been more definite that she's staying.' Lorinda attempted to change the subject. 'The muffin tin isn't ruined, too, is it? It looks a bit warped and out of shape.'

'I don't know what sort of hold she has over him,' Freddie would not be diverted, 'but we've got to break it!'

'How?'

'I'm working on that. We'll think of something.'

'Oh, yes?' Lorinda noted the shifting pronoun. 'And doesn't Macho have any say in the matter?'

'He'll be relieved,' Freddie said airily. 'I don't believe he even likes her any more.'

'Then why does she still have a hold over him?'

'Mmm, good question. Blackmail, perhaps?'

'Macho?' Lorinda had to laugh. 'He's the most law-abiding person I know. What could she blackmail him about? Now, if it were Dorian . . .'

'I take your point, but don't forget that blackout Macho claims to have had the night he and Cressie went out on the town. Something could have happened then.'

'Claims?' But it was just within the bounds of possibility. Either it was a genuine blackout, or something terrible had shocked him so deeply that he had blanked it out and was in denial. But Cressie remembered . . . perhaps had evidence . . .

'You're getting the picture.' Freddie had been watching her face.

'No!' Lorinda shook her head. 'No, I'm not going to believe that. It's only one possible explanation.'

'How many others can you think of?'

'You were here at the time. Were there any media reports of scandals or sinister goings-on that they might have been involved in?'

'Not that I noticed.' Freddie shrugged. 'But I wasn't looking. Whatever it was, it happened in London. If it was just one of the usual drunken brawls, it wouldn't even make the papers. Especially if there were no fatalities.'

'Or it could have been hushed up if there were important people involved,' Lorinda said thoughtfully. 'Politicians . . . or royalty.'

'Politicians, maybe,' Freddie agreed. 'But somehow, I can't quite see Our

Cressie hobnobbing with royalty. Much as she might like to.'

'True, they're not very bookish. She'd have better luck there if she were working with horses.'

'Then there's the editor Cressie was plotting revenge on.' Freddie had another thought. 'Their rocks couldn't reach the twelfth floor, but perhaps Cressie persuaded Macho to go back later and set fire to the building. Even if no one was hurt, the charges would be arson and criminal damage, at the least.'

'Mmmm . . . and that would fit in with those hazy memories of people shouting "Let's get out of here!" Still . . .' Lorinda shook her head. 'No, I can't imagine Macho — even dead drunk — doing a thing like that.'

But-Known appeared to decide that a perfectly good lap was going to waste and leaped up nimbly to settle across Lorinda's knees. Had-I continued to circle Freddie, not giving up hope that something edible might yet be forthcoming.

In the other room, the telephone began to ring.

'Forget it!' Freddie sent an impatient glance in that direction. 'I've had enough for today. Whatever that is, I don't want to know about it.'

With a sound like a hiccup, the phone stopped in mid-ring as the answering machine cut in.

'Freddie — if you're there, please pick up the phone. Please. It's urgent!' The voice, barely recognizable, was ragged with desperation.

'I knew I didn't want to know.' Freddie continued to pour the coffee. 'I suppose the publishers haven't sent the books she ordered, or sent the wrong ones. I wish she'd learn to complain to them and not bother us.'

'Freddie, it's Jennifer — at the bookshop. If you're not there at the moment, then come round to the shop whenever you get in. Please. As soon as you can. The situation is urgent! Almost out of control — No! No, please! Don't do that —' The connection was severed abruptly.

'That doesn't sound like a mis-shipment to me.' Lorinda stood quickly, sending a loudly protesting But-Known tumbling to the floor.

'Oh, all right. I suppose we'd better get over there.' Freddie was curious herself. 'But, I warn you, I'm not up to chasing shoplifters down the High Street.'

At first, the shop looked deserted. The

neat window display was undisturbed and no customers browsed inside. No Jennifer was in sight, either. They entered cautiously.

'No bodies littering the floor, at any rate,' Freddie declared, looking around.

'Perhaps she's in the back room.' Lorinda started forward, still checking for anything that might be out of place.

The large round ball of pale grey fluff curled up beside the till certainly wasn't. As she paused to look behind the counter, it raised its head and blinked pale blue eyes at her.

'Hello, Misty.' She stroked the silky fur and a friendly rumble returned her greeting. A happy contented cat, nothing had upset her recently.

'Over here.' Freddie spoke softly from the doorway to the back room. 'Someone's in here.'

'Is it —' Lorinda found herself tiptoeing over to the doorway to the darkened room. A darker figure could be dimly discerned slumped in an armchair in the corner, surrounded by packing cases.

'Jennifer . . . ?' Freddie called softly. 'Is that you? Are you all right?'

'Don't turn the light on!' Although they were hoping to hear it, Jennifer's voice startled them. 'I have a raging headache.'

'We came as soon as we could.' Freddie pushed the door farther open so that more light filtered into the storeroom. 'Is that all that's wrong?'

'No, of course not. I mean . . .' Jennifer sat up, the damp cloth across her forehead falling into her lap. 'I mean, I'm sorry I disturbed you. It . . . it was a false alarm.'

'Alarm about what?' Lorinda wasn't going to let her off that easily. There had been a tremor of genuine fear in her voice as she pleaded for Freddie to come over quickly.

'It was silly, really, but I panicked. I saw Gemma and her cousin coming along the street with the dogs and, for an awful moment, I was terrified that they were going to come into the shop.'

'Why shouldn't they?' Freddie asked.

'The dogs did seem a bit boisterous today,' Lorinda said, 'but I don't think they'd have bothered Misty.'

'Nothing bothers Misty,' Jennifer said. 'The problem was that Adèle Desparta was already in here.'

'Who?' Freddie looked at her blankly.

'Adèle Desparta . . .' Lorinda frowned, something about the name seemed to ring a dim and distant bell.

'Dorian's guest. Haven't you met her yet?'

'She's only just arrived, hasn't she? I saw a station taxi heading towards Dorian's just a little while ago. There hasn't really been time to meet her.'

'Perhaps not for you,' Jennifer said bitterly, 'but she was around here before she bothered to unpack. I'll bet Dorian put her up to it. She couldn't have known where the bookshop was. He probably drew her a map.'

'But why?' Freddie was still puzzled.

'Because he's been furious with me ever since I included his last book in the remainders sale. He wanted to make trouble.'

'Nothing new about that,' Lorinda observed. 'Personally, I blame Dorian for everything that's happened this past year.'

'No, I mean, why don't you want her in the shop?' Freddie persisted.

'I don't mind her coming in here,' Jennifer said wearily. 'And I don't mind Opal — even though she rearranged my table display to give her book more prominence. But Adèle actually knocked Opal's pile of books off the table while my back was turned — and she tried to blame poor Misty! As though Misty would do a thing like that!'

'Never,' Lorinda agreed. Bookshop cats were all expert at threading their way through stacks of books and even leaping from pile to pile without disturbing a thing.

Prrreow? Misty appeared in the doorway, drawn by the sound of her name.

'No, I didn't call you, darling,' Jennifer told her. 'I was just talking about you and what a good girl you are. Not like some humans I could mention.'

'We've spoiled you, Jennifer,' Freddie said. 'The rest of us are so civilized we wouldn't dream of behaving like that.'

'Well, why should you? You have no reason to. You all write different books with your own separate characters.'

'And they don't? Wait a minute . . .' A distant memory was flickering at the edge of Lorinda's consciousness. Somewhere in the depths of her unexplored souvenirs of the trip was a stack of business cards she had accumulated in her travels. 'What name did you say?'

'Adèle Desparta — and she's in direct competition with Opal Duquette. They're both doing a history-mystery series with Bess of Hardwick as their character!'

'You're right!' Freddie whistled softly. 'Competition doesn't come any more direct than that.'

'I knew I'd met the author of the Bess of Hardwick mysteries in New York!' Lorinda felt vindicated. 'I've even got her business card in my collection. But Gemma said I couldn't have because Opal had never been to New York.'

'That explains why you didn't want them both in the shop at the same time.' Freddie got down to practicalities. 'But what did you think we could do about it? And how long do you think you can keep them apart? They're bound to meet sooner or later, the village isn't that big.'

'I don't know — I thought you could be a buffer zone, or something. I told you I panicked. And I don't care where they meet, so long as it's not here!' Jennifer seemed to be feeling better. 'You should hear the way they talked about each other! I wouldn't like to see them in the butcher's shop, either. The hatchet, the cleaver — and all those long sharp knives lying around . . .' She shuddered.

'Trust Dorian to get us into a situation like this,' Freddie said.

'Dorian couldn't have known that Gemma would have her cousin to visit at the same time.' Lorinda defended him, although she wasn't sure he deserved it.

'Couldn't he?' Freddie quirked an eyebrow. 'I wouldn't put it past him.'

'Anyway . . .' Neither would Lorinda. 'He said she'll be going all over the country doing her research. She may not be here very much.'

'We can but hope.' Freddie did not sound very hopeful. 'We have enough on our hands right now. All we need is another complication.'

Chapter Eight

The rest of the week passed quietly — and without the expected summons from Dorian to any sort of soirée to introduce his guest. In fact, Dorian appeared to be lying low — and there was no further sighting of Adèle Desparta, either.

'Just as well,' Freddie said. 'We can use a quiet interlude before the fur starts flying.'

Prreoh? Had-I appeared to take the comment personally.

'No, not yours.' Freddie offered her a small prawn and then, to preserve the peace, gave one to But-Known. She reached automatically for a third, then sighed. 'Poor Roscoe, it's brutal to keep him under house arrest all the time. I don't suppose you've seen him recently?'

'Not since that nasty trick Cressie played. And I haven't seen Macho, either.'

'I'm not wasting sympathy there, he brought it on himself.'

'Actually, I haven't seen anyone lately.' Lorinda wasn't going to go over that one again. 'I've finally finished all my unpacking and I've been getting some work done.'

'Good for you.' Freddie turned to poke moodily at a saucepan on the electric ring. 'Are there supposed to be lumps in this curry *before* I tip the prawns in?'

'I shouldn't think so.' Lorinda went over to look. It was not only lumpy, it was a peculiar colour, too. And the smell . . . 'Where did you find this recipe?'

'In a very Olde Englishe cookery book. So old I didn't even know what some of the ingredients were, so I took a guess and improvised.' She gave the evil-looking mixture another stir and admitted, 'It may have lost something in the translation.'

'Mmm . . .' Lorinda hesitated, trying to find a delicate way to phrase her suggestion. 'I, uh, think my stomach is still a bit jetlagged. Why don't we just pop over to The Chipper and get some fish and chips?'

'I don't know,' Freddie said reluctantly. 'It seems like giving up.' She picked up the bowl of prawns and held it over the saucepan of alleged curry.

Both cats immediately yowled a horrified protest. Lorinda caught her arm and pulled it back.

'All right, all right, I get the message.' Freddie set the bowl down on the floor instead and stepped back as the cats dived in. 'I suppose you shouldn't waste good food. And —' she scraped the contents of the saucepan into the waste disposal unit, 'you can't win 'em all.'

The Chipper Haddock lurked at the bottom of a turning just off the High Street, masquerading as an Olde Worlde tavern. The spotlighted inn sign swinging above the entrance portrayed a large fish, standing upright on his tail, sporting a bow tie, holding a walking stick in one elongated fin and tipping a straw boater to the advancing customer with the other. Rumour had it that the proprietor had originally intended that the whole should be in neon lights, with the boater being tipped in animation — until the village had risen up in outraged protest. They wanted no neon signs polluting the village atmosphere. An uneasy compromise had been reached with the spotlight, and some villagers still held a grudge against the proprietor for his temerity. It didn't stop them from patronizing the restaurant though: he fried a very good fish.

They paused outside the divided entrance for a brief debate as to whether they wished to turn left for the counter service and order a takeaway to bring home, or to turn right into the low-beamed, dark-panelled dining room and take their meal there.

'Aaah, well met by moonlight, dear ladies!' a voice boomed from behind them. 'Or it would be, if there were any moonlight. How delightful to see you again. Since we obviously have the same aim in mind, may I join you?'

'Please do.' As one and without a consulting glance, they turned right and preceded Professor Borley into the dining room. It was a lot easier to leave a restaurant when one chose, than to try to dislodge a dinner guest at home who was able to ignore any number of hints.

'This is most fortuitous,' Professor Borley said, after they had settled themselves at their table and ordered. 'I had intended to get in touch with you in the next few days, if our paths hadn't crossed before then.' He was looking straight at Lorinda.

'Mmm . . .' she said absently. No doubt about it, this village was too small. Even if it succeeded in expanding into full Town size, it would still be too constricted for its inhabitants to avoid each other.

'Damn!' Freddie said under her breath. Lorinda followed the direction of her gaze to find that Cressie had appeared in the entrance and was looking around, thus proving her point. She averted her gaze hastily, but it was too late. Cressie had spotted them.

'I haven't seen you lately . . .' She came over and hovered pointedly behind the remaining chair. 'Are you expecting anyone else?'

'No, no, please join us.' Professor Borley responded to the hint. 'Is Macho with you? We can always pull up another —'

'He won't be coming.' Cressie's face was grim as she sat down. 'He's too busy working — or so he says!'

'We're all working,' Lorinda said smoothly. 'We have a lot of catching up to do.'

'That's because you've been away,' Cressie said. 'He doesn't have any such excuse.'

'Perhaps he just likes to meet his deadlines.' Freddie's voice was innocent, but everyone knew that there had been rumours about the length of time it had taken before Cressie's last book had been published.

'What are you doing here?' Cressie

counter-attacked. 'I thought you did all your own cooking.'

'Every cook is allowed a night off,' Lorinda said, before Freddie had to confess that tonight's recipe had been a disaster.

The waitress appeared, distracting Cressie's attention. While she was ordering, the door opened again and two more customers came into the restaurant.

'We should have eaten the curry,' Freddie muttered. 'Or at least scrambled a couple of eggs.'

'Lorinda! Freddie!' Dorian greeted them with such enthusiasm that it was apparent that he had been having a difficult time with his house guest. 'And a vacant table for two right beside yours! We *are* in luck!'

Actually, there was a vacant table for two on each side of their table for four. Dorian took the one on the farther side.

'We don't want to sit right next to the door,' he said. 'It keeps opening and the night air is getting a bit chill. We wouldn't want you to catch a cold.'

'You're right, I have far too much to do in the next few weeks to risk a cold,' Adèle Desparta agreed. She smiled vaguely at the others, then frowned. 'Don't I know you? Forgive me, but I meet so many fans.'

'We met at a Mystery Writers of America

meeting in New York,' Lorinda said.

'You two may know each other, but the others have not yet had the pleasure.' Dorian performed the introductions, adding, 'Adèle does the popular series starring Bess of Hardwick Hall.'

'But that's —' Cressie broke off, with the sharp intake of breath and the widened eyes of the suddenly-kicked. Freddie smiled innocently.

'An honour and a pleasure, ma'am.' Professor Borley bowed, unaware of sudden undercurrents. Obviously, he had not yet encountered Gemma's Cousin Opal.

They had reached the restaurant just in time: the dining room was filling up and, beyond the mullioned window panes, Lorinda could see a queue forming for the takeaway. Yes, The Chipper Haddock was a small goldmine, flashing neon sign or not.

'I believe the Specials of the Day are chalked on the blackboard.' As Dorian twisted round in his chair to read them, he had a clear view of the doorway.

Fascinated, Lorinda watched the colour drain out of his face before she, too, turned to see what he was looking at.

Gemma and Opal Duquette had just entered and were peering about for a table.

The only vacant table for two was right beside theirs. Raising her hand in happy greeting, Gemma led the way to it.

'Isn't this nice?' She took the seat against the wall and Opal sat with her back to the room, but facing Adèle Desparta if she looked beyond Professor Borley and Cressie. Neither of them had noticed the other yet.

'Why didn't we take the wall seats?' Freddie mourned. 'Then our backs would be protected when the knives start flying.'

'Be thankful it's a traditional fish restaurant,' Lorinda murmured back. 'Fish knives are too blunt to do much damage.'

'Want to bet? They'd manage to scoop each other's hearts out with a soup spoon, if they got the chance.'

'Just one big happy family,' Professor Borley declared to Gemma in happy obliviousness. 'That's the best part of living in a small place like this, we're all friends and neighbours.'

Cressie looked from one face to another. Freddie shot her a warning glance and, for a wonder, she recognized it and kept her mouth shut. Her eyes were avid, though.

The waitress bustled about with menus and order pad. Everyone smiled vaguely and politely at each other. Dorian engaged Adèle in conversation. Gemma pointed out antiques scattered around the dining room to Opal. Professor Borley ordered more wine and saw that everyone was served. Cressie remained watchful but, thankfully, silent.

'I can't stand it,' Freddie muttered. 'It's like waiting for the other shoe to drop.'

'The first one hasn't dropped yet,' Lorinda said. 'Do you suppose . . .' The idea was coming to her gradually. 'Is it possible they don't recognize each other?'

'Could be . . .' Freddie risked a look at both unconcerned faces. 'If they've never met before. And you know what authors are for using twenty-year-old photos on their jackets.'

'And lots of paperbacks don't have the author's photo at all,' Lorinda said. 'So, if no one introduces them . . .'

'Thank God the English are so bad at introductions. We may just get away with it.'

'Oh, good!' The waitress had reappeared with a large tray and began dealing out the heaped plates of fish and chips. 'I suggest we eat and run.'

'Especially run!' Freddie squeezed her quarter of a lemon with force. 'Oops, sorry!' Juice had squirted across the table at Cressie.

'*Quite* all right!' Cressie's eyes narrowed

as she wiped them. Clearly, she did not believe it was an accident. Freddie would pay for this later.

Just one big happy family. Dorian was simultaneously bolting his food and trying to keep Adèle too engaged in conversation to speak to anyone at adjoining tables. He'd have indigestion tonight — and serve him right!

'Oh, no!' She'd be lucky if she didn't have indigestion herself! Jennifer Lane had just walked in and was heading towards their tables.

Lorinda tried to catch her eye, making little shooing-away gestures. Unfortunately, Jennifer mistook them for a welcoming wave.

'Room for one more?' she asked cheerfully before she looked at the end tables and her smile faded. 'No, perhaps not.' She began backing away.

Too late. 'Plenty of room!' Professor Borley assured her happily. 'Pull up a chair at the end. In fact, we ought to push these tables together and make things more sociable.'

'That does it!' Freddie said. 'I'm leaving!' But it was too late for her, too.

'Yes, *do* join us,' Gemma cooed. 'If I move over, there may even be enough room on the settee.'

'Come over here, Jennifer!' Adèle ordered. 'Dorian, get her a chair!'

'No, really, it will be much too crowded,' Jennifer protested. 'I'll just go next door to the takeaway. I was planning to, anyway, only I saw you through the window . . . some of you . . .' She was floundering. 'That is, I saw Lorinda and Freddie . . . and Dorian . . .' She darted nervous glances at the rivals, who had been sitting with their backs to the windows. She hadn't seen them.

'I don't see any chairs.' Dorian had not turned round to look. 'In any case, I have to get home, I'm expecting an overseas call. She can have my chair.'

'Why didn't I think of that?' Freddie murmured.

'Nonsense!' Adèle wasn't going to let Dorian get away. 'They can call back. I'm not ready to leave yet. I want to have a nice chat with Jennifer. I've thought of several things she can do to improve her shop.'

'I don't think —' Jennifer began.

'That's quite obvious,' Adèle cut in. 'Your layout is much too cluttered. It looks as though you just dumped the books in a pile wherever they happened to be when you unpacked them. Furthermore, you've given far too much display space to general fiction. With so many mystery writers in this area, you should devote more space to them.'

'I've enlarged that section three times since everyone began moving here,' Jennifer defended. 'And —'

'And you're wasting a great deal of space with that non-fiction section. If people want to read non-fiction, they can go to a library.'

'It's a very popular category —' Jennifer began.

'Don't just stand there and take it!' Freddie lost patience. 'Start telling her what's wrong with her books and how she should be writing them.'

'There is nothing wrong with my books!' Adèle turned to face this unexpected attacker, training her guns on Freddie. 'I might, however, be able to tell you what's wrong with yours — if I had ever heard of you!'

'Actually, Freddie outsells you in my shop!' Pushed too far, Jennifer struck back with a note of triumph in her voice. 'So does Opal!'

'Opal?' Adèle quivered, her voice dripping with distaste. 'Opal *who?*'

'Opal Duquette.' Revenge was sweet and

Jennifer was briefly savouring it. 'You know. She does that splendid Bess of Hardwick series. The other one — where Bess is the heroine and not the villainess.'

'My Bess is not a villainess!' Adèle snapped. 'She might be a scheming, occasionally vindictive, bitch — but what choice did she have? She is the prototype of an ambitious modern woman, struggling in a man's world.'

'Elizabeth I was Queen,' Opal said icily. 'So it wasn't *that* much of a man's world. And Bess of Hardwick, kindly and understanding, was one of her closest friends.'

'Hah!' Adèle spat. 'Elizabeth I was the arch-schemer of them all! No wonder they were cronies — or all crones together! They were both cut from the same cloth!'

'*Who* is that stupid woman?' Opal rose out of her chair to glare across the intervening tables. 'And what does she imagine she knows about history?'

'I don't believe you two have met.' Gleefully, Cressie leaped in to make matters worse. 'Adèle Desparta — Opal Duquette. I'm sure you're delighted to meet each other at last. You have so much in common — like the same leading character.'

'I'll bet this is the only time in her life Cressie has ever bothered to introduce anyone,' Freddie noted quietly. 'And she's only done it out of spite!'

'*Common* is one word!' Opal snarled. '*Ignorant* is another! I don't believe that woman has ever opened a history book in her life, far less gone to any source material. Every word she's ever written has been wrong. Worse, an outright lie!'

'I have a degree in history!' Adèle flared back. 'Furthermore, I know how to interpret it correctly. Unlike some little whitewash merchant, who even tries to gloss over murder! Or don't you consider it rather suspicious that three husbands died off so conveniently, allowing her to finally marry the richest and most titled of all?'

'People died earlier then. That first childhood marriage was to a sickly young boy whose illness was already terminal. Her second marriage was very happy and she bore Sir William Cavendish eight children, six of whom survived. He was a lot older and there was never any question but that his death was natural and she mourned him deeply!'

'Perhaps.' Adèle shrugged. 'But it was the third marriage that brought the actual accusation of poison —'

'Lies!' Opal was incandescent. 'All lies — and you're perpetrating them!'

'Opal . . .' Gemma tugged frantically at her cousin's sleeve. 'Opal, sit down. You're making a scene.'

'She's getting plenty of help,' Freddie observed.

'That accusation came from her husband's brother —' Opal's voice rose — 'who was a poisoner himself. Even his own mother knew that he had already killed two people and was now trying to poison Bess and his own brother. She wrote a warning letter to Bess admitting it. Bess was already ill from the poison at the time —'

'One of the oldest tricks in the book!' Adèle's voice rose, trying to drown out Opal's. 'Take a bit to make you sick yourself — or pretend you are —'

'We can have coffee back at the house, Adèle.' Dorian tried to end the situation. Neither woman paid any attention to him.

'If they were cats, you could throw a bucket of cold water over them,' Freddie said helpfully. Dorian rewarded her with a harassed glare.

'Opal!' Agonized, Gemma tugged again. 'Please! People are staring!'

Indeed, they were. Lorinda glanced around to find that their tables had become the centre of the evening's entertainment.

'Let them stare!' Adèle trumpeted, although she had not been the one addressed.

'Oh, dear.' Jennifer Lane began backing away, making apologetic gestures. 'I'm sorry. I didn't mean to start —'

'Is everything all right here?' The manager appeared, their anxious waitress behind him. He was a short stocky man with a nose that bore witness to a past that might have included a stint as a boxer or bouncer. He looked from one to the other of the furious women before him and quailed visibly.

'Perfectly all right,' Dorian said. 'We were just leaving. Charge everything to my account.'

'I'm not finished —' Adèle began.

'Oh, yes, you are!' Dorian caught her arm and pulled her out from behind the table. Lorinda and Freddie exchanged quick glances. The brusque order and rough handling cast an entirely different light on Dorian's relations with his house guest. Mind you, it was nothing they hadn't expected.

'We should be leaving, too.' Gemma, also, intended to brook no further insubordination from her companion.

'What a shame to break up the party,' Professor Borley said. Lorinda shot a startled glance at him, but he was deadly serious.

In the general exodus, the words, 'Too stupid to live!' floated back to them, although it was not clear which woman had spoken. Not that it mattered, since the feeling was obviously mutual.

'I might as well walk along with you.' Cressie had fallen so silent that Lorinda was surprised to find her still there. 'We're going the same way.'

'Come on, then,' Freddie agreed. They all walked with their own thoughts until they reached the High Street when Freddie ventured, 'Quite the little scene tonight, wasn't it?'

'Hmm . . . ?' Cressie had been looking over her shoulder.

'I said —' Freddie gave up. Cressie wasn't listening. She walked beside them, but was not really with them. She seemed to be melting into every shadow along the way and kept peering around uneasily.

'Well!' Freddie looked after her as she said a curt goodnight and darted for the shelter of Macho's house, still taking advantage of every shadow. 'What do you suppose that's all about?'

'Your guess is as good as mine,' Lorinda said.

'And all I wanted,' Freddie mourned, 'was a quiet evening and a meal I hadn't had to cook myself.'

Chapter Nine

Time to pull up the drawbridge and get some work done. In the morning, Lorinda left the answerphone on, didn't open the mail or the newspaper, and resolved to ignore the doorbell if it rang during the day. She could always apologize to anyone who felt slighted later.

The cats were delighted at this turn of events. It signalled to them that life was returning to normal and Lorinda was really going to stay home for a while. They allowed themselves to begin to forgive her defection, so long as she provided frequent cuddles and snacks throughout the day.

Lorinda was happy to oblige. On one of her sorties to the fridge in the afternoon, the doorbell rang and went on ringing insistently. It was a peremptory, *I know you're in there, so you might as well answer* sort of ring and Lorinda would not have felt inclined to respond even if she hadn't resolved to ignore the doorbell all day.

Tiptoeing to the window after the un-welcome would-be visitor had finally given up, Lorinda was not surprised to see Cressie stomping down the path. No one else would have been so rude. Although, now that Adèle and Opal had joined their little group, she was no longer so sure of that.

Nor was she surprised when, checking her telephone calls at the end of a produc-tive day, she found three increasingly plaintive messages from Freddie. This time, she rang back.

'You didn't make the mistake I made,' Freddie said accusingly. 'You were smart enough not to open the door.'

'Cressie?'

'Well, how was I to know? I'm expecting proofs any time now. I thought it was the courier service.'

'Bad luck,' Lorinda sympathized. 'But you won't make that mistake again.'

'You can bank on it! From now on, I look out of the window before I leap to an-swer the doorbell.'

'What's her problem? I take it this wasn't just a social call.'

'That woman doesn't know the meaning of the word social,' Freddie said bitterly.

'She was complaining about Macho. And she wasn't happy about you not answering your door, either.'

'Too bad,' Lorinda said. 'I was working.'

'I was trying to, but she put paid to that. Anyway, come round. Bring the cats, I'm experimenting with chicken liver recipes — that should be right up their alley.'

Had-I and But-Known caught the scent the instant they entered the house and began uttering little yowls of excitement.

'I *did* feed you,' Lorinda reminded them. 'In fact, you've been grazing all day.'

But not on chicken livers! They danced into the kitchen, tails waving, and headed unerringly for the table, where little brown islands dotted a bowl full of curiously pinky liquid.

'Mind your manners!' Lorinda caught Had-I in mid-leap before she reached the table top. But-Known settled for hurling herself at Freddie's ankles, mewling cajolingly.

A tray of bacon-wrapped livers waited to go under the grill. On closer inspection, Lorinda saw that strips of green peppers, halved mushrooms, cocktail onions and chunks of cheddar had been variously secured to the liver pieces by the bacon and skewered by wooden cocktail sticks.

'Looks delicious.' Lorinda discovered that, like the cats, she could easily find room for those succulent titbits.

'Not too enterprising,' Freddie said, 'but it took me a while to get rid of Cressie. I can always get more adventurous another time.'

'I don't know . . .' Lorinda looked dubiously at the bowl on the table. 'That looks rather adventurous to me. We're not going to drink it, are we?'

'Oh that. No. I just read in so many recipes that you soak lamb's liver in milk to take away too strong a taste, that I thought I'd try it with chicken livers and see how it works out. Usually, they tend to go heavily for marinades with chicken livers. I don't know why.'

'Mmm . . . it could be interesting, I suppose.' Lorinda tried to think of a way to suggest to Freddie that, since she wasn't a natural and enthusiastic cook, she might be happier experimenting with a sub-genre other than cooking.

'All *right!*' Freddie rubbed an ankle that had been pricked by impatient claws. 'Wait until it's cooked, can't you?'

'I'm not sure that's necessary,' Lorinda said. 'In their natural state, they eat things raw.' She thought ruefully of dismembered offerings left on the doormat. 'They still do.'

'Not here, they don't. I'm not sure it's good for them. In fact —'

She broke off at the thunderous knocking on the back door. The cats, distracted, moved towards the door.

'Oh, she's not back again!' Freddie cried in exasperation. The knocking did not stop. It sounded as though she was.

'All right, I'm coming!' Freddie threw open the door and Macho stumbled into the kitchen, clutching Roscoe like a life preserver.

'Macho — are you all right?' Lorinda pushed a chair towards him. He looked as though he needed it badly. 'Here, sit down.'

'What's happened?' Freddie demanded. It was clear that something had. There was a large bruise darkening on Macho's forehead, with a dark red smudge in the centre where the skin had been broken.

'I'm quite all right, thank you,' Macho lied gallantly. He slumped in the chair, relaxing his grip on Roscoe, who slid to the floor and rushed to commune with Had-I and But-Known. They touched noses and huddled together, whiskers twitching. Lorinda had the feeling that they were getting a lot more information than she and Freddie were.

She turned back to Macho, surveying him as he gave them his best stiff-upper-lip smile. Two long scratches curved from his left ear to the corner of his mouth. The distance between them exonerated Roscoe from any blame. He couldn't have done it unless he'd used one claw from both paws at once. But Roscoe was a great big softie who never bared his claws to anyone at all, least of all to his beloved Macho. Of course, things were a bit different these days — and if it had been Cressie who had appeared bearing scratches . . .

The scratches hadn't escaped Freddie's notice, either. She looked from them to Lorinda and quirked an eyebrow meaningfully. Definitely, a rift in the lute . . . if there had ever been a lute.

The cats converged on Freddie. Obviously, the exchange of information had gone both ways. Roscoe quivered and let out a plaintive cry.

'He's hungry,' Macho apologized. 'I haven't been able to slip him anything decent all day.' He inhaled deeply and quivered himself. 'There isn't anything decent to slip him. Cressie is making couscous and roasted vegetables for dinner.'

'Then you'd both better fill up here before you go back.' Freddie set the waiting tray of prepared chicken livers under the grill.

'We didn't intend to invite ourselves to dinner,' Macho protested half-heartedly. 'But it looks awfully good,' he added quickly.

'Plenty for all,' Freddie assured him. 'It's not really dinner, but we can bulk it out with some bread and cheese and other bits and pieces I've got in the fridge.'

'It's better than couscous!' Macho spoke from the bottom of his heart. 'Anything is!'

'You're so right.' Freddie's agreement was equally heartfelt. 'Then you can work your passage by opening that bottle of Merlot . . .'

They were just relaxing with their first glass when there were splattering and popping noises from the grill and a cloud of smoke eddied into the kitchen. The cats erupted into hysteria.

'Oh, God — I've got the grill too high!' Freddie was not far behind them. She reached for the handle of the grill pan, burnt herself on it, let go hastily and, snatching up a pot-holder, tried again.

Lorinda rushed forward and turned off

the grill. Macho caught up the tea towel and hurled it over the grill pan to smother the little flames dancing over the bacon wrappings.

'Oh! Oh, damn!' Freddie dropped the grill pan into the sink. 'I should have been paying more attention!'

'No harm done.' Macho raised a corner of the towel cautiously, allowing a cloud of smoke to waft away. 'At least, not much. Personally, I like my bacon good and crispy.'

'It's crispy . . .' Freddie looked down at the smouldering canapés and the charred cocktail sticks holding them together. 'But I'm not sure how good it is.'

'Anything is better than couscous!' The phrase was becoming a mantra for Macho.

'Oh, no!' Lorinda shrieked. The crisis over, she had turned away from the grill to discover a different crisis.

The cats had taken advantage of the humans' distraction to leap on to the table and plunge into the bowl of livers soaking in milk. Three little muzzles were thrust deep into the bowl, three little jaws chomped blissfully, three little tongues slurped up the flavoured milk — and two out of three of the little reprobates belonged to her.

135

'Oh, Freddie,' she wailed, 'I'm sorry. I should have watched them! I'm so sorry.'

'Can't be helped,' Freddie said philosophically. 'We all turned our backs. At least they're enjoying it.'

'It's the first decent meal my poor Roscoe has had in days,' Macho said. 'I owe you a case of champagne.'

'Not necessary,' Freddie assured him. 'He's more than welcome to it. So are yours,' she told Lorinda.

'You'll get it just the same.' Macho shifted from firm to plaintive. 'Er, apart from these . . .' He indicated the burnt offerings. 'They're fine, just well done but . . . you did say you could scrape up a bit more?'

'I'm sure I can.' Freddie opened the fridge door to demonstrate. For once, that elicited no response from the already-feasting cats. 'How about ham and cheese omelettes with lashings of hot buttered toast?'

Macho's eyes lit up, he beamed, then winced. For the first time, Lorinda noticed that he also had a split lip.

'This is like old times,' Macho sighed nostalgically. They were relaxing in the living room, a cat sprawled on the arm of each armchair. Macho, replete and at ease, seemed close to purring himself.

'It wasn't that long ago.' Lorinda tactfully refrained from pointing out that times were still the same for herself and Freddie. It was Macho who was looking back wistfully to the days of BC — Before Cressie.

'It seems like for ever.' Macho rubbed his cheek so forcefully that the scratches began bleeding. Lorinda wondered whether she should mention it.

'You need to put something on those.' Freddie was not so diplomatic. 'They could turn septic if you don't.'

'I don't have anything.' Macho rubbed his cheek again and seemed surprised to find blood on his fingertips. 'I — I — stumbled on the stairs!' he blurted out.

'Quite.' Freddie didn't even pretend to believe him. 'Nasty claws those stair carpets have.'

'Roscoe didn't do it,' he said defensively.

'We never, for a moment, thought he had.' Lorinda spoke for both of them.

'No, really . . .' Having invented a story, Macho was going to stick to it. 'I — I —' He raised a hand to his brow.

'Don't rub your forehead,' Lorinda cut in. 'You'll start that one bleeding, too.'

Too late. A droplet of blood welled up

and rolled down towards his eyebrow, followed by another . . . and another.

'Now you've done it,' Freddie sighed. 'No. Sit still.' She poured a splash of brandy into a glass, dipped the end of her handkerchief into it and began dabbing at the scratches.

'What are you doing?' Macho reared back. 'Ow! That stings!'

'Alcohol is antiseptic,' Freddie said. 'For medicinal purposes in more ways than one.'

'Ow! All right.' Macho winced. 'Just be more careful, can't you?'

'It looks to me as though you should be the one who's more caref—'

The sudden ring of the telephone startled them all. The cats sat up, twitching unhappily. Macho shrank back in his chair. They all seemed to know who it would be.

'Macho is there, isn't he?' Cressie's voice rang out loudly, without preamble. Macho flinched.

'He just left.' Freddie replied to the plea in Macho's eyes. 'I'm not sure where he's gone.'

'You're lying!' It was Freddie's turn to flinch. 'Tell him to get back here right away. It's urgent!' She slammed the phone down and the dial tone began buzzing.

'I heard her.' Macho rose to his feet reluctantly. 'I wouldn't be surprised if the whole neighbourhood did.' He reached for Roscoe.

Mmrrr! Roscoe had heard, too. He dug his claws into the well-padded arm of the chair and flattened himself into it.

'Bear up, old chap.' Gently, Macho disentangled the clutching claws. 'We'll sort something out soon.'

'*Throw* something out,' Freddie muttered beneath her breath. 'And you know who!'

Lorinda nodded agreement. Macho either hadn't heard Freddie, or was pretending he hadn't. Roscoe continued uttering plaintive protests. Had-I and But-Known stared at Macho accusingly, then turned those accusing eyes to Lorinda and Freddie — surely they could do something.

'He can stay, if you like,' Freddie offered. 'For the night, or for a few days.'

'That's kind of you,' Macho said sadly, 'and Roscoe appreciates it. But it wouldn't work. Cressie would know you wouldn't keep him to his diet. She'd just charge over here and take him back. You don't want that.'

'I certainly don't!' Freddie shuddered. 'I

139

had quite enough of her this afternoon.'

'This afternoon?' Macho looked at her sharply. 'What —'

The telephone began to ring again. Macho wasn't moving fast enough to suit Cressie.

'Tell her I'm on my way.' Cradling Roscoe, he turned and left through the kitchen.

As soon as he opened the back door, the phone stopped ringing. Cressie must have been watching the house.

'Of all the people I've ever known,' Lorinda said wonderingly, 'I'd never have cast Macho Magee in the role of a hen-pecked boyfriend.'

'If his fans could see him now,' Freddie agreed.

'And there's nothing we can do about it?' Lorinda looked at her helplessly.

'Frankly, I'm beginning to lose patience with him,' Freddie said. 'I'm inclining to the view that he got himself into it — and I'm afraid he's going to have to get himself out of it.'

'He got poor Roscoe into it, too. That isn't fair.'

'That's our only hope,' Freddie said. 'So far, Macho has been willing to put up with her inflicting that awful diet on Roscoe but, if she ever tried to treat Roscoe the way she's treated him, he might start to do something.'

'He might even hit her back.' Lorinda found the idea appealing.

'That would be too much to hope for,' Freddie said regretfully.

Chapter Ten

During the next few days, Macho never left his house. To all intents and purposes, he had disappeared from view. Unfortunately, the same couldn't be said for the other inhabitants of Brimful Coffers.

Lorinda recognized that she was scaling new heights in her endeavours to sidestep, evade and escape her colleagues and fellow villagers. It wasn't until she dropped into the library that morning that she discovered she wasn't the only one.

'Oh, it's only you.' Honor Norton, the librarian, appeared suddenly from an alcove, relief in her voice and a smile on her face. A library assistant also hove into sight and the hitherto deserted reception desk resumed its busy workaday life.

'Only me,' Lorinda confirmed. 'Why? Who were you trying to avoid?' As though she couldn't guess the answer.

'Not you,' Honor said. 'You're all right

but . . .' She looked towards the entrance nervously. 'We have to be just a little bit careful about visiting authors these days.'

'Trouble?' Lorinda asked sympathetically.

'Oh, nothing we can't handle.' Honor grimaced. 'But we'd rather not. We do hate scenes.'

Lorinda couldn't fault them on that. She had begun to notice that she was not the only person in the village who had taken to loitering outside shops until she'd had a good look through the windows and assured herself that neither of the warring rivals was inside.

'I hope Macho Magee is all right,' Honor said. 'We haven't seen him around lately.'

'I'm sure he's fine,' Lorinda assured her smoothly. He was probably keeping out of sight until his scars faded. 'I haven't seen much of him myself. He's . . . very busy.'

'Oh, yes.' The sharp glance let her know that she wasn't getting away with anything. '*She's* been in. Borrowing some very strange books on his card.'

'Strange?' Lorinda wondered uneasily what Honor thought of her own selection. Perhaps it was better not to know.

A sudden flurry of protesting yelps and yaps erupted outside the entrance to the library.

'Oh, dear,' Honor said. 'Gemma's hitching them to the railings. They hate that. They'll be fussing all the time she's in here.' She watched the door nervously. 'Is she alone?'

She was. Gemma hurried through the doorway, looking back over her shoulder, and came to a sudden halt at the desk.

'Oh!' She seemed surprised to find herself there. And more surprised to find them. 'Oh!' She shook her head groggily. 'Oh, how nice to see you again. You must be well recovered from your trip now.' She gave Lorinda a weak smile. 'You're looking so rested. And so well.'

The same couldn't be said of her. The word that sprang to mind was 'haggard', followed by 'harassed' and . . . 'hunted'?

'Hello, Gemma. Um . . . are you by yourself?' Honor was looking a bit harried herself, still watching the door as though she suspected a trick to lull her into a false sense of security.

'Oh, it's so peaceful here!' Gemma leaned against the desk, unmindful of the patrons beginning to glare in her direction. Obviously, she did not hear the noise her own dogs were making to disturb the peace of others.

'I'm glad you think so.' Honor's lips tightened. She looked towards the disturbance outside and back at Gemma. Her expression changed abruptly. 'Gemma, are you all right?'

'Yes, yes.' Gemma pulled herself away from the desk and stood there swaying. 'I'm fine.'

'You're sure?' Lorinda moved closer to catch her if, as seemed all too likely, she fell. 'You look a bit —' She stopped abruptly, before the word 'haggard' actually escaped. 'A bit tired,' she finished.

'Oh . . . yes, well, I must admit I haven't been sleeping too well lately. Too much . . . disruption . . .'

'You mean Opal works late at night?' Lorinda was prepared to sympathize — up to a point. She often worked late at night herself, although she could see it might be disturbing to another person in the house.

'Oh, no, Opal isn't any bother . . . that way. She's still at the research stage in her new book, so that just means a lot of reading. Very quiet and no trouble to anyone . . .'

But there was something wrong. Gemma was trying to smile now — and not making a very good job of it. Honor was still watching her with concern. Patrons collapsing in the library presented a tricky situation when one had to decide quickly whether it was necessary to call an ambulance or whether a short lie-down in the staff lounge would be sufficient.

'Oh!' Gemma jumped suddenly. 'What's that?'

'What's what?' Honor frowned; hallucinations definitely required an ambulance.

'The dogs . . .' They had stopped barking. Only Gemma was upset by the silence.

'Someone must be fussing over them, that's all.' Honor assured her from long experience of dogs parked outside and susceptible villagers stopping to admire them.

'Oh, yes, I suppose so.' Gemma seemed unconvinced. 'But perhaps I ought to make sure they're all right . . .'

The barking started again before she reached the door and Freddie entered on a wave of outraged howls. How dare she leave them and go into the building that had swallowed up their mistress?

Freddie swept up to the desk, dropping her armload of books on to it. They were all cookbooks, Lorinda noticed.

'Ooooh . . .' Gemma craned her neck to read the titles. 'Planning a party?'

'Not with this little lot.' Freddie pushed them across the desk to Honor for cancelling. 'I'll have a look around for something more . . . challenging, I think.'

'You know where they are,' Honor said. 'Good luck.'

'What are you —' Gemma began, but Freddie sent an imploring look to Honor.

'Or perhaps you'd like to have a look in the stacks.' Honor interpreted the look correctly. 'We have a lot of very old books there, waiting to be repaired or deaccessioned. You might find something of interest.'

'Perhaps I could help.' Gemma stepped forward eagerly. 'If you tell me what you have in mind . . .'

'Sorry.' Honor did not need another look from Freddie. 'Only one member of the public in the stacks at a time. Library rule.'

'Thanks!' Freddie said gratefully and fled.

'Oh, well . . .' Gemma looked after her plaintively. 'I was only trying to be helpful.'

'I'm afraid Freddie is in the throes of inspiration.' Lorinda hoped she wasn't fanning the flames of Gemma's curiosity. 'She's at the point where no one can really help her. She has to work it out for herself.'

'Oh, you creative people!' Gemma shook her head. 'How well I know! Life at the magazine would have been so simple, if it hadn't been for you.'

There wouldn't have been a magazine, if it hadn't been for them. Lorinda forbore to point this out, but her exchange of glances with Honor was eloquent.

'Just remember —' Gemma shook her finger at them coyly. 'If you ever do need any help, you can call on me.'

A cold day in hell, was the cliché that sprang to mind, but Lorinda kept her face smooth. 'I'll tell Freddie that.' Her voice was even smoother. 'I'm sure she'll appreciate it.'

'Any time,' Gemma assured her. 'Any time at all.'

'Right . . .' Lorinda gathered up her issued books, piled them into her shopping cart and left the library, carefully skirting the exuberant Lionheart and Conqueror, who obviously felt that she should pause and entertain them for a while.

It was a pleasant day, with just a hint of impending rain, which might or might not arrive before nightfall. She had no menu planned, she'd just see what looked good in the shops. It was so lovely to be home and able to arrange her own meals and days, without having to fit into everyone else's plans for her.

Lorinda stopped smiling as she reached the crossroads and the makeshift shrine. There was something different about it. She realized that the flowers that had been gently fading away had been replaced by fresh blooms. Not all of them. The bouquets at the base of the lamp post were still withering and dying inside their dusty cellophane carapaces. It was the bouquets at eye level and above that had been renewed — a poignant reminder that parents, relatives and close friends were still grieving, unwilling to allow the memory of the dead child to fade into oblivion along with the flowers.

More poignantly still, some of the miniature toys dotted about amongst the bouquets were also losing their identity after being battered by rain and wind, their tattered ribbons holding them to the post by only a few last frayed threads.

Grave goods. Reminders of things cherished in this life to accompany the departed one into the next, providing comfort and memories of love on the journey. How the race memories of ancestral beliefs lingered.

Her eyes blurred by sudden tears,

Lorinda turned away. The day no longer seemed so promising. As that other day must have done — to a child, every day is promising. That it might be the day of their own extinction was undreamt of.

'So sad, isn't it?' Betty Alvin fell into step beside her. Where had she come from? Lorinda had not seen her approach. It was not the first time Betty had appeared unexpectedly at this place. Did she spend much time hovering by the shrine?

'That poor family will never get over it, you know,' Betty continued. 'Everyone says how fortunate they are to have another little girl and a boy, but it's not the same, is it? They've still lost a child, with its own personality and hopes and dreams, no matter how many other children they have.'

Lorinda murmured agreement and was relieved when Betty's chatter moved on to lighter items of local gossip. They parted amicably — and to Lorinda's relief — at the fishmonger's.

'Couple of lovely heads of cod and haddock I've put by for your lucky cats,' he greeted her. 'Boil 'em up until the flesh falls off the bones and you've got a feast fit for a king — and almost good enough for your lot.'

Lorinda laughed and allowed him to add

the fish heads to her order. The cats would appreciate them, even if the preparation was messy and a bit gruesome. She owed Had-I and But-Known a bit more pampering to help atone for what they considered her gross desertion.

She encountered a bemused Professor Borley at the greengrocer's.

'Sprouts,' he complained, looking to her for elucidation. 'Brussels sprouts — we don't have them where I come from. And these Jerusalem artichokes.' He gestured towards the small knobbly tubers in an adjoining bin. 'What on earth do you do with these?'

'Avoid them, mostly.' Lorinda laid it on the line. 'Unless you're planning to be on your own for the next twenty-four hours or so. They're very gas-producing — about equal to three tins of baked beans.'

'Is that a fact?' He looked at her oddly, suspecting mockery. 'Then why do they have them?'

'They're quite tasty and they make a delicious soup. But you don't find it on the menu very often because a lot of people feel that it isn't worth the consequences.'

'Hmmm . . .' He dropped the tuber he had been inspecting back into its bin and moved on hastily. 'Maybe I'll just have a bunch of carrots, instead.'

'That would be safer,' Lorinda agreed, selecting spring onions, beetroot and baking potatoes. 'It doesn't always pay to be too adventurous.'

'You've been to dinner at Freddie's since you got back,' he deduced gloomily. 'I hope you had better luck than I had.'

'It wasn't really dinner,' Lorinda confessed. 'It was more of an assortment of canapés. Most of them were quite good.'

'You did have better luck.' He nodded resignedly. 'I got something that was supposed to be Japanese. At least she won't put that recipe in her book. She'd lose a lot of readers, if she did. Maybe permanently. I wouldn't be surprised if it proved fatal to anyone of a weak disposition.'

'Good heavens! What did she give you?'

'I don't know and I don't want to know. I just don't think I'll be accepting any more dinner invitations from her for a good long while. Nothing personal, you understand, just self-preservation.'

Lorinda made a mental note to find out exactly what Freddie had concocted that had had such a traumatizing effect on Professor Borley. It might be a useful recipe to have in her armoury if he became too intrusive.

'Oh, yes.' As an afterthought, she added a bag of plump tempting lemons to her basket of purchases.

'I like lemons,' he said wistfully. 'But, if I buy that many, they shrivel up before I get a chance to use them all. Maybe I should do more entertaining.'

'What you should do —' How had he reached the age he had and still remained so unaware of basic principles? — 'is simply squeeze them all at once, strain the juice into an ice cube tray and freeze it. Then you have lemon juice on tap whenever you want it. No fuss, no muss, no bother.'

'You don't say?' He snatched up a bag of lemons eagerly. 'I never thought of that.'

'Just bear in mind,' she warned, 'they don't pop out as easily as ice cubes. I'm not sure why. You may have to coax them out with the tip of a knife, but it's still a lot easier than squeezing it from the start, especially if you have guests waiting.'

'I will, indeed, remember that.' He beamed at her. 'I'm learning a lot more than I expected to on this sabbatical. I'll bet,' he added wistfully, 'you're a lot better cook than Freddie.'

'We all have our specialities.' Ignoring the hint, she moved towards the cash register, hoping he would not follow. It was a vain hope, she realized.

He was still at her heels when she stopped short at the door and retreated so quickly that she backed into him. She couldn't help it. Gemma had caught up with her and was just walking past the shop.

'I'm so sorry,' she apologized. 'I just remembered I want some —' She looked around frantically for something at the very back of the shop she could possibly use. 'Some celery!' she finished triumphantly, making a dash for it.

'I understand.' Again, he was right behind her. 'I don't want to meet the lady, either. I'm afraid I might be a bit sharp with her. We've had some disturbed nights at Coffers Court since her cousin came to stay.'

'Oh?' This time he had caught her interest. 'Wild parties? Or late night working?'

'Nothing so mundane.' He shook his head. 'I'm not sure what's going on, but it seems to involve doors slamming in the small hours of the morning and muted hysterics — but not muted enough.'

'Oh, dear. No wonder Gemma is looking rather awful.'

'She is, indeed, and I have every sympathy. But,' he added with the innate canniness of a long-term veteran of academic wars, 'I don't want to get involved.'

'Actually,' Lorinda agreed, 'neither do I. I have far too much work to catch up with. I can't afford to be distracted.'

Chapter Eleven

She might have been able to discourage Professor Borley, but the members of her own close circle were another matter. Unfortunately, it now appeared that Cressie considered herself one of them.

'Hello?' The voice on the other end of the line held a strange quiver that Lorinda instinctively felt boded no good. 'Lorinda? Are you there? Please, please, tell me you're there.'

'Cressie?' Lorinda asked uncertainly. 'Is that you?' Why, oh why, hadn't she left the answerphone on to screen incoming calls? 'What's the matter?'

'Matter?' Cressie gave what was obviously meant to be a light laugh. It sounded more like a creaking hinge. 'Why should anything be the matter? I just thought I'd like to come over and have a little chat with you.'

'You mean . . . right now?'

'If you don't mind.' It was not like Cressie to sound so unsure of herself. For that matter, it was most unlike her to telephone first instead of just arriving on the doorstep. And she had even said please.

'Actually . . .' Lorinda thought quickly. 'I was just on my way over to Freddie's for tea. Why don't you join me there?' She wasn't going to face this alone.

'Oh . . . all right.' Cressie seemed reluctant.

'In about twenty minutes,' Lorinda instructed firmly. That would give her time to fill Freddie in on the situation.

'Yes. Oh, by the way . . .' Cressie was elaborately casual. 'Is Macho there with you?'

'Macho? No. I haven't seen him for days. Why?' But Cressie had rung off.

Lorinda replaced the phone and went for her coat. The cats were instantly at her feet, as though sensing her destination. Or perhaps they had recognized Freddie's name.

'It's all right, I was going to ring and invite you round anyway,' Freddie said, as Lorinda finished her explanation. 'I wasn't planning on Cressie, but I daresay we'll manage. Food seems to be the least of her preoccupations.'

'I'm sorry,' Lorinda said, 'but —'

'No apologies necessary. I quite under-stand. I wouldn't want to be landed with her on my own, either. Or is Macho with her?'

'No. In fact, she asked if he was with me. I don't think she knows where he is.'

'Done a runner, has he?' Freddie smirked. 'Not before time, I'd say. I'm only surprised it's taken him this long to get around to it.'

'If he has, he's gone about it the wrong way. He should have remained in his house and got rid of her.'

'Well, that's Macho for you.' Freddie shrugged. 'Always going about things the wrong way round. Haven't you ever won-dered why all these meek little men write the rough-tough-shove-another-grapefruit-in-her-face books? Sheer wish-fulfilment, that's what it is.'

The doorbell pealed sharply, startling them both.

'I told her twenty minutes,' Lorinda said indignantly. 'It can't be more than ten.'

'Why the front door?' Freddie started to-wards it. 'She's not usually so formal — and the back door is closer.'

The cats watched with narrowed eyes. Lorinda saw Had-I's back begin to arch and But-Known's fur bristle, so she was not entirely unprepared for the flurry of yaps and yelps as Freddie opened the door.

'I'm sorry to drop in on you like this,' Gemma said, 'but I was just passing and it occurred to me —'

'Come in.' Freddie's voice was resigned: she led the way into the kitchen. The cats hissed, informing the intruders that they considered this part of their territory.

The pugs yelped again, as much at the sudden clatter at the back door as at the cats. Gemma tried vainly to quiet them.

'I'll get it.' Lorinda opened the back door and Cressie darted inside, setting off a fresh paroxysm of hysteria from the pugs.

'You're not going to unleash those, are you?' Cressie stared at the dogs coldly.

'No, no,' Gemma denied hastily, tugging back on the leashes. 'We're not staying. We're out for our walkies. I only popped in for a moment to ask — That is . . . I was wondering . . .'

'Yes?' Freddie tried to hurry her along.

'Wondering if you've seen Opal today? She was gone when I got up this morning. And she didn't come back for lunch. And she didn't leave a note, or anything . . .'

'Are you still looking for Macho?' That

reminded Lorinda of Cressie's earlier concern.

'Isn't he here?' Cressie looked around suspiciously.

'Well, well,' Freddie said. 'So we have two missing persons. Perhaps they've run off together.'

'Oh, I'm sure not —' Gemma began. 'Oh. Oh, I see. You're just having your little joke.'

'That isn't funny!' Cressie snapped.

'It wasn't intended to be.' Freddie widened her eyes in improbable innocence. 'It was just a helpful suggestion.'

'How long has it been since you've seen Macho?' Lorinda tried to keep them to the point. So far as she knew, Macho hadn't been sighted in any of his usual haunts for at least a week. This could be serious.

'Since yesterday afternoon. We were wor— just having a quiet discussion when he threw a book across the room and stormed out. And . . . he hasn't come back . . . yet. He has a filthy temper!'

'Not usually,' Lorinda murmured. 'He's the most patient and kindest of men.'

'That just shows how little you know him,' Cressie said. 'He has no patience at all. It's almost impossible to get a civil word out of him. And all he cares about is that bloody cat!'

They didn't need Freddie's snort to emphasize the fact that Cressie would try the patience of a saint.

'Where *is* Roscoe?' Lorinda was not to be sidetracked. 'Did he take him with him?'

'I wish he had! The damned thing won't stop yowling and it's driving me crazy!'

'Then Macho won't stay away long.' Lorinda gave a long sigh of relief. 'He wouldn't abandon Roscoe.'

'No? And what about me? I suppose it's all right if he leaves me high and dry? Just when we're at a crucial point! Just when I most need —'

She broke off abruptly. It was probably the expression on Gemma's face that had stopped her.

'Unless something has happened to him,' Gemma said darkly.

'What — What do you mean?' Cressie went pale.

'Macho would never abandon his cat, just as I'd never leave my dogs. Unless I couldn't help it. Unless — An accident can happen to anyone.' Gemma rubbed her forehead, as though trying to erase a memory. 'That poor child — I'll never forget it. And yet, I can't remember enough. I keep feeling . . . There might have been something I saw . . . Without actually registering it consciously. I think, I really do think, I ought to try hypnosis. They say it can help you recover buried memories.'

'You want to be careful if you're going to experiment with that,' Freddie warned. 'It might regress you right past the accident and into previous lives you've lived.'

'That's right!' Cressie's attention was caught. 'I've heard of that. People go right back into history and discover all sorts of things about themselves and the historical period. It would be a natural for your cousin Opal, too.'

'Oh, I don't think Opal would agree to —' Gemma began.

'We could all try it!' Cressie's eyes gleamed. 'We could have a party and hire a hypnotist to regress us all.'

'Oh, I don't think . . .' Gemma's protests were growing weaker. 'Everyone . . . That's a bit excessive . . . I was thinking of a private consultation. You . . . You're turning it into a game.'

'It would be a great party!' Cressie steamrollered over her. 'Everyone could come in costume. A Come-As-Who-You-Think-You-Were Party! Then the hypnotist could regress them and they'd find out if they were right.'

'It would certainly be different,' Freddie said.

'It would be wilder than a Botox Party!' Cressie had the bit in her teeth and was not to be stopped. 'And think of the publicity! We'd all gets lots of publicity. I might even be able to get that TV show interested.'

She probably would, although how much publicity would accrue to anyone but Cressie was a debatable point. She was wiser than the others in the ways of the soundbite. And Lorinda wouldn't put it past her to fake her own regression into a more glamorous era. She made a mental bet with herself that Cressie was another Cleopatra wannabe. Or possibly Catherine the Great.

'I'm not really sure Macho would approve of this,' Lorinda said tentatively.

'Oh, yes, he will.' Cressie's jaw set stubbornly; she was not to be discouraged. 'I guarantee it!'

'I wouldn't want publicity,' Gemma demurred, blissfully unaware that little of it was likely to fall her way. 'I just want to help that poor family to come to some sort of resolution of their grief. Closure, I believe it's called now, although I don't believe such tragedies can ever be closed.'

'What?' Cressie looked at her blankly, having obviously forgotten the reason for her inspiration. 'Oh, yes. Yes, you can try. That would make great copy, too. Especially if you could come up with something solid. A name . . . or even a registration number.'

In which case, Gemma would definitely get her share of the publicity. Lorinda watched her absorb the idea.

'Do you ever have the feeling that things are getting out of hand?' Freddie asked, *sotto voce*.

'Almost constantly — when Cressie is around,' Lorinda replied.

'Macho will put a stop to this when he comes back.' Freddie looked at her in sudden doubt. 'Won't he?'

'I don't know,' Lorinda said. *If he comes back.* But he wouldn't leave poor Roscoe as a hostage to fortune, would he? Or was he trusting to her to look after him?

'. . . and it's so beautifully photogenic.' Cressie was concentrating her blandishments on Gemma now. 'I understand you people use it for your parties a lot. That gorgeous reception room they've made out of the old banking hall — *so* much nicer than any of this . . .' She flicked her fingers in a disparaging gesture that dismissed any venue that Freddie, Macho or Lorinda could provide.

'Well, it's a thought . . .' Gemma was being persuaded.

'Coffers Court looks so luxurious.' Cressie was pressing hard. 'And that's the impression we want to convey. Opulence, luxury — all so photogenic, telegenic — it will come over beautifully.'

'What about the Manor House?' Freddie put in. 'That's even more luxurious and photogenic. What's wrong with Dorian's place?'

'In a word, Dorian.' Cressie wrinkled her nose, possibly trying to get it back into joint. 'How much publicity do you think any of you would get if we used his Manor? He'd be swanning around, acting as host, grabbing all the camera angles. No, we need a more neutral venue, like Coffers Court.'

'I do see your point,' Gemma said. 'And I'm sure the other Court residents would agree.'

'Why shouldn't they? They're all going to be invited. It will be very convenient for them — all they have to do is step out of their flats and they're at the party.'

'It *has* been a long time since we've had a big party,' Gemma said wistfully. 'And we used to have such nice ones.'

'This will be the best of all,' Cressie promised.

'And if . . . nothing happens . . . when he hypnotizes me, then it won't seem so important because all of the rest of you will have your turn and no one will notice so much.'

'That's it!' Cressie beamed on her like a teacher encouraging a backward pupil. 'You needn't worry about a thing. Everyone will —'

Hhhhsssss! A loud snarling hiss from But-Known interrupted them. As one, they turned to see But-Known advancing in fury upon Conqueror, who was in the process of lifting his leg against a corner of Freddie's stove.

'Stop that! Stop that at once!' Alerted, Freddie stormed forward, hand upraised to clout the offending pug.

'Oh, no! Oh, dear!' Gemma tugged at the leash. 'I'm so sorry! We were going walkies. He must be — It's not his fault. He didn't mean —'

She broke off as Lionheart advanced, sniffed briefly and began to raise his own leg.

'No! No!' She jerked the leashes frantically. 'We're just leaving! We shouldn't have stopped! I'm so sorry —' She dashed for the back door and found Freddie there ahead of her, opening it.

'Oh! Thank you.' The pugs strained at their leashes, pulling her off balance and nearly toppling her. 'I'll talk to you later,' she threw over her shoulder to Cressie, as the dogs raced for the nearest tree.

'Have I ever told you —' Freddie closed the door and looked down at Had-I and But-Known — 'just how much I appreciate your cats?'

'They have a lot to recommend them.'

'I guess they do.' Even Cressie had to agree. 'But, I'm not sure . . .' She looked at them uneasily. 'Just what do you do about a litter box? Macho always took care of that.'

'Personally,' Lorinda ventured, 'I have a cat flap and I just leave them to it. They only use the litter box when the weather is exceptionally bad.'

'Oh.' The answer obviously did not please Cressie. 'But that means letting him out. And then some people —' Her accusing gaze swept over them. 'Irresponsible people — will feed him and ruin his diet.'

'Better than letting him die of starvation,' Freddie said.

'You wanted to talk to me?' Lorinda forestalled Cressie's reply. 'Some sort of problem, it seemed?'

'No.' Cressie looked away. 'No, not at all. It was just a thought. It doesn't matter now. I ought to be getting back and — Oh!' Something in the distance caught her eye. 'There's Macho now!' She rushed to the door. 'I must catch him before . . .' She was gone.

' "Before he gets away again", was the ending of that sentence, I think.' Freddie watched through the window as Cressie intercepted Macho at his own front door and an obviously heated altercation began. 'Now what are we to make of that?'

Chapter Twelve

The young woman walked briskly down the street, her head high, her eyes bright, the sun glinting on her newly coiffed blonde hair. She had been in the hairdresser's for longer than usual today, but the results were worth it. She'd had a manicure, too, her nails delicately shaped and glowing red. Red. All ready for her important date tonight. She was young, beautiful, self-assured, striding towards happily-ever-after.

Unsuspecting.

The head was waiting for her in her bedroom closet.

Gift-wrapped. With a perky bright red bow.

Sooner or later, she would find it. When, didn't matter. It would keep.

Rather — a long whinnying snicker escaped him — it wouldn't keep.

The red blood pooling into the bottom

of the plastic bag beneath the pretty wrapping would darken and turn brown. The face would darken, too, and begin to dissolve. If she hadn't found it before, she would find it then.

When it began to smell.

Even then, she would not imagine the reality. The bright expensive wrapping would fool her into thinking it was an overlooked gift. Perhaps one that had been put into her closet to surprise her.

A basket of fruit, perhaps. Gone rotten because not discovered in time. Guiltily, she would begin to open it, perhaps tearing at the wrapping, hoping to find a card from her well-wisher.

The head was his calling card.

Then she would know. Or begin to know.

The second head — the one that was draining in his bathroom sink now — would convince her.

Especially when she recognized them. One by one, her best friends were going to be returned to her in pieces.

And she would know it was going to happen to her, too.

Soon.

And slowly. He had learned a lot since that first amateur effort. He could keep them alive a lot longer now, while he . . .

Lorinda squinted her eyes to blur the type and checked the pages to the end of the chapter. Twelve pages of gut-wrenching detail as the killer reminisced.

She hoped the editor hadn't been trying to digest his lunch when he read them. On second thought, she hoped he had. It would serve him right. Except that he was probably so hardened to this sort of thing that he wouldn't notice how sickening it was. Or perhaps it was a she — some of the worst of them seemed to be edited by women. What did they have against their own sex? And the more gruesome the book, the bigger the advertising budget it seemed to attract. *New York Times Best Seller List* was emblazoned across the cover, just above the title. No wonder Macho got so upset, there was no justice!

And where was Macho? She had witnessed his not-so-rapturous reunion with Cressie yesterday and had expected him to have dropped over — or, at least, telephoned — by now. Of course, it was still early, not quite noon, although you couldn't tell that from the darkness outside.

Another grey gloomy day — well, it suited the mood the book had put her into.

Lorinda hurled the paperback across the room so violently that it bounced off the opposite wall before dropping into the waste basket below, narrowly missing But-Known.

'Come back, darling!' Lorinda called, as the cat skittered out of the room. 'I'm sorry. I didn't mean it for you. It's all right. Come back . . .'

It took minutes of coaxing before the small head poked cautiously around the door frame. By this time, Had-I, attracted by the dulcet tones, behind which lurked the promise of impending treats, was also on the scene. She paused, communed briefly with But-Known and led the way over to Lorinda. They sat at her feet and looked up at her expectantly.

'Oh, all right.' She gave in, leading them kitchenwards. 'I think we still have some munchies in the cupboard.'

They looked with disfavour at the thin stream of munchies that trickled into their bowl.

'I'm sorry,' Lorinda said. 'I thought we had more than that. I'll get a fresh supply when I'm out shopping tomorrow. Can't you make do with these for now?'

They gave her a haughty look and stalked across to the back door, staring pointedly towards Freddie's house.

'She isn't home,' Lorinda told them. 'I saw her leaving this morning. She took the car, so there's no telling when she'll be back.'

That wasn't good enough, they let her know. Furthermore, they had no intention of using the cat flap. The least she could do was open the door for them.

'All right.' She opened the door. 'Go and see for yourselves.'

To add insult to injury, it began to rain. They stopped on the doorstep and stared at her accusingly.

'Honestly, it isn't my fault,' she said, as the first splattering of drops rapidly became a heavy downpour. 'I had nothing to do with it.'

Disbelievingly, they turned as one and marched back across the kitchen and into the living room. When she checked on them a few minutes later, she found them, as she had expected, curled up together in a corner of the couch and fast asleep.

They had the right idea. The rain was teeming down now, with no promise of a let-up. The best thing to do with this sort of day might be to sleep through it.

Of course, that option wasn't open to everyone. Through the front window, she saw Gemma battling her way down the High Street, struggling with dogs, umbrella and . . . yes, Cousin Opal. They appeared to be arguing.

Briefly, Lorinda wondered if Opal really had been off somewhere with Macho yesterday when Gemma and Cressie were looking for them. That would be amusing, she thought, and abruptly realized that she wasn't so amused at all.

Cressie would be incandescent. The thought cheered her for a moment. And yet, why shouldn't Macho, a former history teacher, want to spend some time with a colleague who was an historical novelist? They must have a great deal in common. Perhaps Opal was even consulting him on some aspect of the Tudor era. If anyone knew most of the ins-and-outs of that particular period, it would be Macho.

As she watched, Opal drew herself up and snapped something obviously offensive at Gemma, who also drew herself up as far as was possible with the dogs tugging at their leashes and keeping her off balance.

Opal stamped off and Gemma stumbled her way to the nearest lamp post where there was a long pause while the pugs occupied themselves and Gemma rootled in her bag for the pooper-scooper. Her umbrella tilted as she did so and a trickle of icy water found its way between the collar of her raincoat and her neck. She shuddered visibly.

'You may have your drawbacks,' Lorinda turned away from the window and addressed the sleeping cats, 'but I wouldn't swap you for that lot.'

Had-I twitched in acknowledgement before burying her nose deeper between her front paws. But-Known opened one lazy eye and shut it again in what might have been a conspiratorial wink.

There was a sudden telltale clunk from the kitchen. The cats heard it, too, and raised their heads, abruptly alert.

'What do you want to bet?' she asked them. They uncurled themselves, leaped to the floor and followed her into the kitchen.

Sure enough, a wet bedraggled Roscoe was crouched by the feeding bowl, gulping down the munchies Had-I and But-Known had so recently despised. Of course, now that someone else wanted them, they were changing their minds. They advanced upon Roscoe, determined to remind him just whose territory this was.

'Poor baby, you're drenched.' Lorinda tore off some paper towels and proceeded to blot Roscoe. He gave a rusty purr, but was not to be distracted from his purpose. He didn't lift his head until the bowl was empty. Then he looked around for more.

Lorinda watched the door expectantly. If Roscoe had arrived, could Macho be far behind?

She set out another cup and saucer, but the afternoon wore on and there was still no sign of Macho. She went back to work, while Roscoe, having eaten everything available, joined in as the cats resumed their interrupted nap.

The rain settled into a steady downpour, eliminating the temptation to do anything other than work — except, perhaps join the cats in their nap. Along about what would have been twilight, had there been any brighter light at all that day, she heard the sound of Freddie's car returning.

She was not surprised when, after a suitable interval — long enough for shopping to be unpacked and stowed away — the telephone rang.

'I may go mad!' It was not the voice she expected to hear. In fact, it was one she would have considered most unlikely.

'What's the matter, Dorian?' She refrained from saying that, whatever it was, he had probably brought it on himself.

'Adèle! Adèle Desparta! She's driving me out of my mind!'

'Oh?' Yes, he had definitely brought it on himself. 'Perhaps you ought to get together with Gemma. I gather she's having rather a difficult time with Opal. You can commiserate with each other.'

'God forbid!' he snarled. 'Gemma and that damned cousin of hers are the problem where Adèle is concerned. It would be more than my life is worth to go near either of them. Adèle would kill me!'

'I suspect that Opal would take exception to Gemma talking to you, too. She'd think it was consorting with the enemy. It's a shame they both had to visit at the same time.'

'This town isn't big enough for both of them,' Dorian agreed. 'And I'd rather not be around for the shoot-out.'

'How much longer is she staying?'

'Who knows?' She could hear his shudder over the phone. 'How much longer is Gemma's cousin staying?' he asked hopefully.

'I gather she may sublet Rhylla's flat for the summer. She's staying with Gemma while she considers it.'

'Hmm . . . pity.' Abruptly, he changed tack. 'Anyway, why don't you come up and have a drink?'

'What?' She looked at the waterfall streaming down the window panes. 'You mean . . . now?'

'No time like the present. Come along,' he coaxed. 'You've done enough work for one day. Come and relax.'

And take some of the strain of entertaining his tiresome guest, he meant.

'Actually . . .' She stretched the truth a bit. 'I was just going over to Freddie's.'

'Bring her along.' He sounded slightly desperate. 'The more, the merrier.'

'She's very busy.' Freddie would be no more enthusiastic than she was about trudging through this downpour to pull Dorian's chestnuts out of the fire he had, as usual, lighted himself.

'Oh, but all work and no play . . . You need a break . . . refresh yourselves . . .' He was close to babbling.

'Not today.' The rain drumming against the windows helped her to stand firm. 'Honestly, Dorian, another time.'

'Oh, come along. I'll open the jar of caviar my Russian publisher sent me . . .'

The offer might have tempted the cats, but Lorinda was able to resist it. She recognized Dorian's magnanimity however. He really must be desperate. For a moment, she had thought he was actually going to utter the word 'please'.

'Just for a few minutes . . . half an hour . . . and I'll . . . I'll . . .' Somewhere in the distance behind him, a door slammed loudly. 'Oh, very well then —' His voice changed. 'I see I can't persuade you, so we'll make it another time.'

'Adèle has just gone out,' Lorinda surmised.

'Er . . . actually, yes. And —' his voice brightened even more — 'she's getting into that car she hired. That means she'll be gone for some time, perhaps the rest of the day.'

'Congratulations —' But he had already rung off.

Lorinda shrugged and replaced her own receiver. It was only a temporary reprieve, but it was better than nothing. And next time he issued an invitation, the weather might be better.

The yawn caught her by surprise, just as she was wondering whether or not to ring Freddie and suggest a drink.

That settled it. She didn't really want to go out in this monsoon, not even the short distance to Freddie's house. Nor would it be kind to make Freddie venture out again into the storm.

The cats had the right idea: a cat nap.

Chapter Thirteen

When she woke it was pitch-black outside and still raining, but not so heavily.

She turned on the lights and was closing the curtains when a flicker of movement at the far end of the front path caught her attention.

Someone was out there. Someone who had hastily stepped back into the shadows when she had appeared at the window. Someone who did not want to be seen?

Frowning, she pulled the curtains together and turned to the still-sleepy cats, who were just beginning to stir and stretch. Only Roscoe was reluctant to move: he remained in a tightly curled ball and opened one wary eye.

'It's all right,' Lorinda told him. 'I wouldn't turn you out into a night like this. You can stay until Macho comes to collect you.' In fact, he could stay the night. She wasn't going to ring and tell anyone where he was.

Perhaps it had been Cressie lurking outside, coming to peek through the window to see if Roscoe — and perhaps Macho — was here. It seemed like the sort of thing Cressie would do.

The curious thing was that Macho had not come looking for him. Or had Macho disappeared again, first freeing Roscoe to seek a refuge of his own?

The cats followed her into the kitchen where, feeling a bit foolish, she crossed to look out of the window before turning on the light. The back garden held no skulking form and the view over Macho's and Freddie's gardens showed them to be empty and peaceful.

She was just opening the fridge door when she froze. The cats heard the sound, too. They turned towards the back door, fur bristling as the sound came again. Someone was scratching at the door.

She started for the door slowly, telling herself not to be silly. It was probably only Macho, come to reclaim his cat. If so, why was Roscoe's fur beginning to stand on end? And why didn't Macho just knock?

They all converged silently at the door. Lorinda stared helplessly at the doorknob, waiting to see it turn.

'Macho . . . ?' she called tentatively. 'Macho . . . is that you?'

The scratching came again . . . and . . . a snuffling noise.

'Macho . . . ?' Suppose he were lying there, wounded in some way, unable to call out. The sounds seemed to be at the base of the door.

A low rumbling growl came from Roscoe's throat. It was not Macho out there.

On the other side of the door, the scratching became more insistent.

'Go away . . .' Lorinda said faintly. She backed away from the door, looking around for a weapon before she —

No! Be sensible. There were wiser ways to handle this situation than opening the door to go rushing out, weapon or not, into the unknown. She wasn't going to behave like the victim in one of those paperbacks she had brought back. She went to the phone and dialled briskly.

'Freddie? Listen — can you take your phone to the window? I'll turn on the light over my back door and you can tell me what you see there.'

'Right!' Freddie said. 'Don't bother with explanations. I just love guessing games.'

'There's something odd going on. I think

someone is at the back door . . . or something . . .'

'All right, I'm at the window,' Freddie said. 'Turn on the light.'

Lorinda put down the receiver and hurried back to the kitchen. As soon as she snapped the light switch, any report from Freddie became unnecessary.

Sudden yelps, yaps and an outbreak of canine hysteria told her what was on the other side of the door — and explained those unsettling snuffling noises. Encouraged by the light, the pugs howled to be let in, forepaws thudding against the door as they hurled themselves at it.

On the kitchen side, the cats ranged themselves for battle, snarling and spitting curses at all dogs who would dare to encroach on their territory.

'Gemma?' Why hadn't she said anything? 'Gemma, are you all right?' Lorinda opened the door. It was a mistake. The cats shot forward as though jet-propelled, clawing and howling. The pugs yelped, yipped and tried to stand their ground before being forced into ignominious noisy retreat, the cats chasing after them, equally noisy.

'I must say —' Freddie, raincoat flung over her head and shoulders, appeared in the doorway — 'having you back has certainly livened up the neighbourhood.'

'But where's Gemma?' Lorinda was squinting into the darkness, which brightened as another door opened and light streamed from that source. Macho and Cressie peered out to see what all the commotion was about.

'That's right.' Freddie was looking around, too. 'Where is she? You don't suppose those rotten beasties have knocked her off her pins again and left her lying in a puddle? I wouldn't put it past them.'

'Here, Roscoe . . .' Macho bleated into the night after his unheeding cat. 'Here, Roscoe! Come to Daddy . . .'

'Eeeyuch!' Cressie made retching noises. 'You and that damned cat! How can —'

'Gemma,' Lorinda said loudly. 'We must find Gemma. She could be hurt.'

'Gemma?' Macho was called back to order. He snatched up an umbrella from the stand inside his door and hurried to join them.

'Where *is* Gemma?' Cressie was trailing after him, struggling into a waterproof poncho. 'I thought she never let her darling pooches roam about on their own.'

'You're getting the picture,' Freddie applauded. 'Gemma isn't here — and the dogs are. She's missing and we're all there is for a Search Party — so let's start searching!'

'We could follow the pugs,' Lorinda suggested. 'If only the cats would stop chasing them. They might lead us to her.'

'I don't believe you people!' Cressie shook her head. 'You're unreal!'

'You've got a better idea?' Freddie challenged. 'Speak up — do give us the benefit of your wisdom. We'd love to hear it.'

'Cressie — shut up!' Macho ordered. 'Either come with us or go back to the house and — and —'

'I'm coming!' Cressie snapped. '*You* shut up!' She hurried after them as they headed towards the High Street. 'Don't go so fast — wait for me!'

At the border of what they considered their personal territory, the cats suddenly seemed to notice that it was raining and they were getting wet. They peeled off and turned back towards warmth, food and shelter.

The pugs, still feeling pursued, although by two-legged tormentors rather than feline enemies, continued on their way. They were making for Coffers Court now and running faster as their goal came into sight.

Only for a brief moment did they pause to sniff at a huddled heap of rags, lying half in the gutter and half on the pavement as they came close to their destination. Dismissing it as of no importance, they resumed their flight.

The humans halted and remained staring down at the sodden bundle of cloth which, as their eyes adjusted to the darkness, gradually revealed that it was bunched around a still form.

Uncaring, the pugs raced off.

'Well,' Freddie said. 'I guess we've found Gemma.'

'Guess again.' Macho was bending over the inert body. 'This is Cousin Opal.'

'She looks . . . she looks . . .' Cressie faltered. 'Is she . . . dead?'

'That's for the experts to say.' Macho tried to position his umbrella on the pavement to belatedly shield the body from the rain. 'But . . .'

It was not long before the sound of an ambulance whooping through the night once again disturbed the peace of Brimful Coffers.

'It's my fault!' Gemma wailed. 'It's all my fault!'

'Nonsense,' Macho said, 'you didn't kill

her.' Then ruined it by adding, 'Did you?'

'Of course not! Not that way — but I sent her out to walk the dogs.' Gemma fondled the pugs distractedly. 'She didn't want to do it — but I'd walked them this afternoon and I got so wet . . . I felt a chill coming on. I was afraid it would turn into a streaming cold, if I went out again. But the dogs had to be walked —'

'It's not your fault,' Lorinda soothed, more thankful than ever for her cats. 'You couldn't have known this would happen.'

'But what's so awful —' Gemma would not be comforted. — 'is . . . is that I lost my temper with her when she tried to get out of doing it. I told her she ought to start pulling her weight and doing something useful, rather than just sitting around complaining about Adèle. I . . . I almost shouted at her. I . . . I sent her to her death!'

'Here.' Freddie thrust a drink into Gemma's hand. 'Get this down you!'

'Oh, but I've already had — Oh, what does it matter!' Gemma accepted the fresh drink and took a big gulp. 'I should have gone out with the dogs myself. Opal didn't know the terrain, the places where the kerb is extra-steep, where the holes in the road are. And . . . and sometimes the dogs can be a bit hard to control. Especially if you're not used to them.' She took another gulp and coughed. 'Oh, that *is* strong!'

'It's meant to be,' Freddie said. 'And when you've finished that, you'll have another. And another. The only thing your friends can do for you now is knock you out until morning.'

'Oh, you *are* kind,' Gemma sighed. 'But, you know, Opal and I weren't really that close. It's the shock — and I feel terrible because I feel so guilty. But really, we were more like casual friends than close relatives. I was really surprised when she contacted me to ask about properties in Brimful Coffers. Of course —' she preened herself briefly — 'word *is* getting around that this is *the* place to live, if you're in the mystery world. But, before that, we hadn't seen each other in years. And then only at family reunions. The family —' She took a huge gulp and choked again. 'I'll have to tell them —'

'Time enough in the morning.' Freddie patted her shoulder consolingly and looked across to Lorinda. 'Shall I stay with her tonight — or will you?'

'No, no!' Gemma gasped. 'That isn't necessary. You've done quite enough . . .

so kind . . . I'm sure I'll sleep . . . probably.'

'Cressie will stay,' Macho volunteered recklessly.

'Now wait a minute —' Cressie protested.

'Really,' Gemma demurred weakly, accepting a fresh drink. 'She doesn't have to —'

'Oh, yes, she does.' Macho fixed Cressie with the sort of cold stare that carried a hundred unspoken messages — none of them pleasant.

'Oh, all right,' Cressie said ungraciously, glaring back at Macho.

'You'll sleep better tonight,' Lorinda said, 'knowing that Cressie is here.'

'So will Macho,' Cressie sneered.

'I wish you wouldn't . . .' Gemma's protests were growing weaker. 'You mustn't all worry about me. I'm quite all . . .' Her head dropped against the cushions abruptly and her just-emptied glass fell to the floor.

The pugs whimpered and sniffed anxiously at her face. Then, assured that she was only unconscious, settled down — one on each side of her — to get some sleep themselves.

Lorinda watched and forgave them their seemingly callous desertion of Opal. They had obviously realized that nothing could be done to help her — and besides, she was not Gemma. She meant little to them.

'You're not staying there,' Freddie told them. 'And neither is she. As for you —' She turned to Cressie. 'We'll put Gemma to bed and leave the night light on. All you'll have to do is look in on her occasionally and make sure she's all right.'

'Macho?' Cressie looked to him uncertainly. 'Macho — you're not really going to leave me here alone?'

'You're a big girl now,' Freddie answered before Macho could weaken. 'You've made your reputation — such as it is — by insisting on that. Now prove it. After all,' she added maliciously, 'it's not as though we were asking you to sit up with the corpse, is it?'

'Oh!' Cressie lost colour at the thought — what price her posturing with Angostura bitters now?

'Come along.' Lorinda stepped forward to take Gemma's other arm as Freddie levered her out of the armchair, murmuring soothingly. 'Time for beddie-byes.'

'I'll take her.' Macho caught Gemma's limp form and half dragged, half carried her into the bedroom.

It was, Lorinda suspected, easier for him

than staying in the living room and facing Cressie's recriminations. The suspicion was reinforced when, having dumped Gemma on her bed, he remained in the bedroom, turning his back like a gentleman while she and Freddie undressed Gemma, put her into a nightgown and settled the duvet over her.

When they left the bedroom, Macho was close on their heels, as though moving in convoy.

'I don't think she'll wake,' Freddie told Cressie. 'But, if she does, just top her up with the scotch. That will send her off again.'

'But . . .' Cressie looked to Macho again, unwilling to believe he was deserting her.

'I'll see you in the morning,' he said. '*Late* morning,' he added pointedly. In a most ungentlemanly way — for him — he was the first one out of the door, leaving Freddie and Lorinda to follow behind.

'Let's have a peaceful nightcap at my place,' Lorinda invited. 'Although I'm afraid I don't have any nibbles to go with it.'

'Come to me,' Freddie counter-invited. 'I have plenty of snacks.'

'Ah, but *I* have a cat flap!' Lorinda played her trump card.

'Roscoe!' Macho rose to the bait. 'He'll be there?'

'He's been there all day,' Lorinda said. 'I was expecting you to follow him. Where were . . .'

But Macho had dashed ahead to wait impatiently at the front door. The moment Lorinda unlocked it, he pushed past her and was the first into the hallway.

'Roscoe?' he called. 'Roscoe, where are you?'

Had-I and But-Known strolled out to greet everyone, giving Macho a supercilious look, and followed them into the living room, prowling hopefully while Lorinda fixed the drinks.

'Where's Roscoe?' she asked. It was obvious they knew. They looked at her blandly and turned away, their ears flicking in the feline equivalent of a shrug.

'He's probably hiding out until he's sure that Cressie isn't with you,' Freddie said. 'And who can blame him?'

'I don't know why you have it in for her.' Macho was defensive. 'She's not *that* bad.'

'Try telling that to Roscoe,' Freddie said.

'Speaking of telling —' Lorinda wrenched them back to a sterner reality — 'who's going to tell Gemma what really happened? Gemma seems to be under the impression that Opal fell and hit her head.'

'The police,' Macho said firmly. 'It's their job.'

'If Cressie doesn't shoot her mouth off during the night,' Freddie said.

'That's why we stayed until Gemma passed out,' Macho reminded them. 'She isn't going to surface for a long time. Cressie may get bored keeping vigil, but she won't get the chance to liven things up by telling tales, because Gemma is out for the count.'

'Let's just hope she stays that way,' Freddie said. 'She isn't going to take it well when she learns it was another hit-and-run. She's still upset enough about the first one.'

'Accidents *do* happen.' Lorinda wondered which of them she was trying to convince — perhaps herself. 'And in the same place — or close to it. That's why they call them accident black spots.'

'Mmm-hmm . . .' Freddie said. 'And lightning can strike twice in same place. Maybe even three or four times, but —'

'I don't know why we're even talking about this! It's going to be up to the police to —' Macho's tetchiness disappeared as a large furry ginger head materialized from seemingly nowhere and stroked itself against his ankles.

'Roscoe!' He bent and scooped the cat out from under the chair and into his arms. 'There you are!'

Roscoe looked around warily before allowing himself to relax cautiously into Macho's embrace. The enemy might not be in sight, but he still wasn't sure that she was not nearby.

'It's all right, boy, it's all right,' Macho soothed. 'She isn't here, she won't be back tonight. Our home is our own again — and I've got a nice tin of tuna hidden away for you.' He lurched to his feet and started for the door.

'Don't you want to finish your drink first?' Freddie suggested.

'Eh?' Macho turned towards her blindly before registering the question. 'Oh, no, no. Perfectly all right. I have plenty at home, if I want it. In fact,' he rubbed Roscoe's ears, 'we're getting ourselves a secret little cache of goodies — just for Roscoe and me. Don't worry about us.' In a sudden swift movement, he was at the door — and was gone.

'Well!' Freddie was the first to recover. ' "I got plenty of nothin' ", if you ask me.'

'I didn't.' Lorinda looked at the closed

door. 'But let's have another drink ourselves.'

'Pity . . .' Freddie accepted her refreshed
glass. 'For a moment there, back at
Gemma's, I thought the worm was turning.'

'Macho's not a worm . . .' Lorinda did
not sound quite convincing. 'Not really.'

Chapter Fourteen

Lorinda had been vaguely surprised when the police arrived on her doorstep in the morning, but realized that some form of statement must be required from anyone who found a body. Even though she could tell them nothing; whatever had happened had happened long before she and the others had arrived on the scene. Heaven knew how long the dogs had been snuffling around the village before they came to her back door, presumably because they had often visited her with Gemma and hoped to find Gemma there.

The police had been sympathetic, re-assured her that they hadn't really ex-pected her to be able to tell them a great deal, and gone on to interview Freddie.

She was not surprised when, shortly thereafter, Freddie appeared at the kitchen door, slumped into a chair at the table and reached out desperately for the cup of coffee Lorinda was prompt in serving.

'*That* was a workout!' Freddie said. 'And yet it wasn't half the grilling I've put some of my characters through in my books. It wasn't a grilling at all, they were really rather sweet. So why do I feel as though I've just gone six rounds with Chris Eubank?'

'Because it's happening to you. We don't expect that sort of thing to happen to us personally.'

'Well, it's happening to Macho and Cressie now.' Freddie spoke with grim satisfaction. 'And I'll bet they'll have a rougher time of it, if Cressie can't keep a civil tongue in her head.'

'I'd better make more coffee.' Lorinda made no move towards doing so, there was plenty of time. The police had just left Freddie.

She was unprepared for the imperious rap at the back door and amazed when Dorian rushed into the room as she opened the door.

'Did you tell them?' he demanded. 'What have you said to them?'

'Tell who what?' Lorinda stared at him in blank amazement.

'You're referring to the police, I assume.' Freddie, not so dumbstruck, was quicker on the uptake.

'They've just been here, haven't they?'

Dorian looked around anxiously, as though a constable or two might still be lurking in some corner.

'Relax,' Freddie said, 'they've moved on. They're putting Macho and Cressie through their paces now.'

'Oh? Oh, that's all right then. They don't know anything. It was you —' he gave Lorinda an accusing look — 'you, I confided in.'

He made it sound as though they'd been exchanging their darkest secrets, sealed with an oath of blood. Lorinda mimed a baffled shrug in response to Freddie's raised eyebrow.

'We were discussing it just yesterday!' The asperity in Dorian's tone said that surely she couldn't have forgotten something so vital. 'On the telephone. When we agreed that this town wasn't big enough for the two of them — and we didn't want to be around for the shoot-out.'

'Oh!' Light dawned. 'Oh, but we were just —'

'It was already too late,' he said portentously. 'Now they've had their shoot-out — and Opal lost.'

'You don't think —' Lorinda began.

'Hang on —' Freddie was struggling to keep up.

'You can't imagine that Adèle had anything to do with Opal's accident! That's —'

'*If* you remember,' Dorian said nastily, 'Adèle went out while we were talking on the phone. She took the car she'd hired — and she didn't return until well after midnight. You didn't tell the police that, did you?'

'How could I? I had no idea how long your house guest stayed out. Why should I? It was nothing to do with me. Believe me, Adèle Desparta's whereabouts were the last thing on my mind last night.'

'Wait a minute.' Freddie was still trying to catch up. 'Are you telling us that you seriously suspect Adèle of —'

'You never heard the way she kept ranting about Opal Duquette's interpretation of Bess of Hardwick and her motives. All day, every day. The woman had no other subject of conversation. She was obsessed. Fit to kill. And I don't know what she expected me to do about it. Tar and feathers and riding Opal out of town on a rail weren't in it.'

'Even so, that's a pretty serious —'

'I have good reason.' He cut Lorinda off short. 'I went out and inspected her hire car this morning. There was a large dent in the front right-hand bumper!'

'Do you mean to tell us —' Freddie stared at him unbelievingly. 'You actually suspect your guest — your friend — of murder?'

'The thought had crossed my mind,' Dorian said with great dignity. 'After all, she hated the woman.'

'But it was an accident,' Lorinda said. 'A dark, wet night, a skid, a —'

'And after you introduced that killer into our midst last year.' Freddie was relentless.

'That was very unfortunate, I admit. But it could have happened to anyone. And I suffered more than anyone — he nearly killed me. And he destroyed my aquarium and all my precious exotic fish. I don't know why you're taking that tone with me. I am more to be pitied than censured.'

'A killer last year — and now you think you've got another killer in your house this year. Dorian —' Freddie shook her head — 'you sure can pick 'em!'

'Never mind that!' Dorian snapped. 'Just make sure neither of you breathe a word of this to the police.'

'I wouldn't dream of it,' Lorinda assured him. 'It's all hearsay and supposition. They wouldn't have a leg to stand on if they tried to make a case out of it.'

'That's right,' Freddie said. 'For instance, did you inspect that hire car when it arrived? That dent you're worried about could have been there all along. Some of these hire cars get pretty hard usage.'

'I am not a garage mechanic!' Dorian said huffily. 'Why should I go around inspecting cars?'

'You did this morning.'

'That's different. This morning I had grounds for suspicion.'

'Or a wild imagination. Just because you're regretting your invitation to her that's no excuse for wanting her marched out of your life in handcuffs.'

'That's the last thing I want!' Dorian glared at Freddie. 'I've already told you, I don't want a whisper of this to reach the police!'

Lorinda had stepped back from the fray. Through the window, she saw the police walking away from Macho's at a leisurely pace. One of them said something and the other one laughed. No problems there.

She started the fresh pot of coffee and it was just beginning to perk when the expected knock sounded at the door.

'What kept you?' Freddie raised her cup to Macho and Cressie as they entered.

'Nothing.' Macho was tight-lipped.

'What are *you* doing here?' Cressie did a

double-take at sighting Dorian. 'I didn't think you socialized.'

Dorian winced. 'I was just passing,' he said, 'and I thought I'd drop in and ask if there was anything I could do.'

'Aren't you in the wrong house?' Cressie put her finger on the flaw in this excuse. 'All we did was discover the body. It's Gemma who should get the sympathy.'

'I'm on my way there now.' Dorian rose with dignity. 'Poor Gemma must be quite distraught.'

'I'll bet that's more than you can say about Adèle.' Cressie eyed him shrewdly. 'You must have had a hard time keeping her from dancing in the street.'

'What —' Dorian collapsed back into his chair. 'What makes you say that?'

'No more competition.' Cressie shrugged. 'The field is clear for her now.'

'Who —' Dorian glared around accusingly. 'Who told you that?'

'All those two did was slag each other off every chance they got. It isn't rocket science to know they'd love to see each other dead. And now it's happened.' Cressie had reached the obvious conclusion. 'So, did she do it?'

'Do what?' Dorian was still fighting a rearguard action. 'I don't know what you're talking about. And, whatever it is, I hope you haven't mentioned it to the police.'

'I don't mention anything to the police.' Cressie's voice was cold.

'Keep it that way.' Dorian's tone was equally icy. He pushed himself upright and, this time, stayed that way. 'I'll get along to Gemma's now and see if there's anything I can do. Although —' he looked around pointedly — 'it's really more of a woman's job.'

'That's a sexist remark!' Cressie snapped.

'I'm doing the traditional thing,' Freddie assured him. 'I have a casserole in the oven for Gemma, I'll bring it along when it's cooked and had time to cool down.'

'I'm glad *someone* knows the proper thing to do.' Dorian was almost at the door; he did not look back. 'It makes a nice change!' The door slammed behind him.

'That snotty bastard!' Cressie raged. 'I don't know why you put up with him!'

'He isn't so bad,' Macho said.

'Oh, yes, he is — and so are you!' Cressie turned on him. 'You and your Macho Magee!'

Macho gave a low wordless growl that set the cats looking around to see if Roscoe had joined the group.

'If you're doing that,' Lorinda had been considering the matter, 'I suppose I should do something about flowers.'

'Just don't tie them to a lamp post,' Freddie said. 'We don't want any more shrines around here.'

'No use saying that.' Macho had lapsed back into gloom. 'Some fool is bound to start one.'

'I didn't think anyone cared enough about her to bother,' Cressie said.

'That isn't the point,' Macho said. 'A person has died, that's all anyone can do to show respect.'

'No — Freddie's right.' Cressie sounded surprised to find herself agreeing with anyone. 'We don't want any more shrines. The High Street will begin to look like Murder Mile!'

'Stop bleating about murder!' Freddie snapped. 'Who said anything about murder?'

'So, why do *you* think the police were swarming all over us?' Cressie faced her defiantly.

'They have to investigate fatal accidents —' Macho began.

'Accident?' Cressie challenged him. 'The second hit-and-run in two months?'

'Vehicular homicide is what they call it

in the States.' Lorinda recalled newspaper stories in one of the cities she had briefly visited.

'Exactly! The first hit might have been someone else's accident, but I'll bet it gave Adèle the idea when she heard about it. What a way —' Cressie grew wistful — 'to get rid of your rival!'

'Stop that!' Macho twitched nervously. 'Stop insinuating that Adèle —'

'It's what Dorian thinks!' Cressie had them there; they could not deny it. 'Why else is he so nervous about what we might have told the police?'

'Dorian has an over-active imagination,' Lorinda placated. 'We all have. That's why we're writers and not accountants or secretaries.'

'That may be so.' Cressie was going down fighting. 'But it's pretty bloody convenient for her to have a clear field. Bess of Hardwick is hers alone now — and she'll pick up Opal's readers, too.'

'She probably has them already,' Lorinda said. 'A lot of readers would be fascinated to see how their two opposing views handled the same historical situation.'

'True.' Freddie nodded. 'I was rather looking forward to when they got to the time when Bess and her fourth husband had to act as hosts/jailers to Mary, Queen of Scots.'

'Now you'll get the one unopposed version,' Cressie sniffed. 'Too bad it wasn't the other one who was killed. If Opal had been quicker off the mark, she could have done away with Adèle instead.'

'It's not a game!' Lorinda suddenly felt that she had had quite enough of Cressie. 'The woman is dead.'

'That much is indisputable.' Macho took Cressie's arm and began urging her towards the door. He, at least, had realized that she had worn out her welcome.

'I hope you didn't say any of this to Gemma last night.' Freddie eyed her with direst suspicion.

'I couldn't. She never woke up until morning. She might have slept even longer, but those dogs began making such a fuss they woke her. I couldn't keep them quiet.'

'Did you try taking them for a walk?' Lorinda asked. 'That was probably what they wanted.'

'Or feeding them?' Freddie suggested.

'Walk? . . . Feed?' Cressie looked at them blankly, they might have been speaking an alien language.

'Cressie doesn't really understand the concept of food,' Macho said bleakly.

'All your pets are overfed.' Cressie glanced scornfully at the innocent Had-I and But-Known, who were a perfectly respectable size. 'It's amazing that they can still waddle around.'

'Better than being too weak from hunger to walk at all!' Lorinda leapt to the defence of her cats.

'You can't think very well when you're hungry, either,' Macho said.

'All right, all right!' Freddie cracked under the subtle pressure. 'Come round to me for dinner tomorrow — all of you. Just remember — I'll be experimenting.'

'Your experiments are better than —' A sharp thump in the middle of Macho's back sent him reeling through the door Cressie had just opened. It slammed behind them.

'That's torn it!' Freddie said. 'I shouldn't have done that.'

'Oh, yes, you should,' Lorinda said firmly. 'Did you see how Macho's poor face lit up at the prospect of a good meal? He probably hasn't had one in days.'

'Unless that's where he'd gone when Cressie came looking for him,' Freddie speculated. 'Sneaked off to a restaurant in Marketown, where she couldn't catch him.'

'Too bad he couldn't take Roscoe with him,' Lorinda sighed. 'I wonder how much longer he can put up with it. And why?'

'I wonder why that car couldn't have hit Cressie instead of Opal.' Freddie shook her head. 'Why is it always the wrong person who gets killed?'

Chapter Fifteen

'Oh, how kind of you.' Gemma accepted the casserole and looked at it helplessly, as though she didn't know what to do with it. 'How very, very kind.'

'And something for dessert.' Lorinda proffered the lemon meringue pie she had picked up at the bakery along the way. She had decided, upon reflection, that it would be less emotive than flowers and, certainly, no one could tie it to a lamp post. 'Sorry I didn't have time to bake it myself.' She still felt a bit guilty about that.

'Here, I'll take that.' Betty Alvin emerged from the kitchen and relieved Gemma of the casserole. Gemma looked around even more helplessly, then stepped forward to take the pie from Lorinda and pass it to Betty.

'So kind, so very kind,' she repeated. 'Everyone is being so very kind.'

'Naturally. Everyone rallies round at a

time like this.' Professor Borley appeared in the living-room doorway, brandishing a cocktail shaker. 'How about a drink?'

'Oh, I'm sorry!' Gemma was flustered. 'Do come in and have a drink. I should have asked you . . .'

'It's all right.' The professor draped an arm across Gemma's shoulders. 'No one is standing on ceremony at a time like this. They understand.' He frowned. 'It just seems a shame that there seem to be so many times like this in our little village.'

'It's not that little,' Freddie said, as they followed him back into the living room. 'There are too many new people moving in these days.'

'Oh, how true!' Gemma said. 'It's that new housing development on the other side of the hill. It's bringing in all manner of new people — not our sort, at all.'

'That's progress, I suppose,' the professor sighed.

'We don't want that much progress here,' Gemma said petulantly. 'They're inflating property prices, swamping the schools with their children, turning the village into just another dormitory community for London. And the place is crowded with their horrid builders driving around in those nasty white vans with ladders on the roof.

And they all drive through the village much too recklessly . . .' Her voice faltered. 'And too fast.'

Awareness of the reason they were all there abruptly swept over them. Gemma blinked back tears.

'Sit down, Gemma.' Lorinda eased her into an armchair. 'Where are the dogs?' It was the most comforting thing she could think of to say.

'I shut them in the bedroom. There are so many people . . . coming and going . . . I was afraid they'd get outside . . . and . . .'

'Here you are!' Professor Borley deftly twisted the cocktail shaker open and poured a cheerful red fluid into a glass. 'Wrap yourself around that. It will help.'

'Thank you . . . Oh, that's delicious! What is it?'

'One of my specialities.' He beamed and looked at the others. 'Anyone else for a Moonraker?'

'Why not?' Freddie and Lorinda accepted their glasses and sipped appreciatively.

'Not bad.' Freddie nodded. 'What's in it?'

'Very simple. One-third brandy, one-third Dubonnet and one-third peach brandy or liqueur — either works well.

Then . . .' He chuckled. 'Then, the recipe book — it was a translated Continental one I found in an old bookshop — called for three jiggers of Pernod!'

'Good Lord!' Freddie said. 'There's never that in here?'

'Of course not.' He chuckled again. 'You should have seen some of the other recipes: they told you to use three jiggers of Angostura bitters on top of all the other regular ingredients. Once I'd run across that a few times, it was easy to figure out what must have happened. The translator obviously thought that a jigger was the same as a dash.'

'It sounds as though the editor was asleep at the switch,' Lorinda said. 'Or perhaps not such a linguist, either.'

'I tell you, I've had quite a few laughs out of that book. But, once I got the hang of the recipes and used dashes of Pernod, or bitters, or whatever else they'd measured in jiggers, quite a lot of the drinks were very good. Interesting use of some different liquors, too. I was surprised at the number using Dubonnet. In our countries, nobody seems to do anything much with it but splash some gin into it.'

'I must admit —' Gemma held out her glass for a refill — 'I *do* like a spot of gin and Dubonnet myself. And I understand it was the Queen Mother's favourite tipple. But I could be converted to this quite easily. In fact, I think I already am.'

'So am I.' Professor Borley drained the shaker into her glass. 'Oops! Time to mix another batch. I'm assuming —' he looked at the others — 'you're all game for another round?'

'We are,' Lorinda said. 'And Betty will have one, too.' Betty had just come in bearing a tray of clean glasses she had obviously been washing in the kitchen.

'If it's not too much trouble,' Betty said.

'Nothing easier. I could mix it in my sleep. Brandy, Dubonnet and peach.' He poured them into the shaker and chortled. 'And three jiggers of Pernod.' Carefully, he measured out the dashes. 'No wonder that book had the telltale streaks across the top that meant that it had been remaindered.'

'Remaindered!' Freddie shuddered. 'It should have been pulped!'

'Now, now,' he chided. 'I'd have lost a lot of laughs, if I'd never found it. Besides, anyone who knows anything would never have followed those instructions.'

'But suppose it fell into the hands of someone who didn't know?' Betty said.

'Then they'd have learned at the first

gulp,' he chuckled heartlessly. 'If they had any taste buds left after that.'

His booming laugh startled the pugs into action; first, the hysterical yapping, then the dull thuds as they hurled themselves against the locked door. They didn't want to stay shut away in there — they wanted out, *out,* OUT!

'Oh, dear,' Gemma said. 'They want to go walkies.' She shrank back into the chair, losing colour. 'They want walkies — and . . . I can't . . . I can't!' She huddled in the chair and burst into sobs.

'Take it easy,' Freddie said. 'Take it easy.'

Lorinda patted her shoulder ineffectually.

Professor Borley refilled her glass.

The yapping went on. It was not going to stop. Some instinct told the pugs that they were being heard, that they were the centre of attention. The demanding yelps increased in volume.

'Oh . . .' Gemma pulled herself together and tried to struggle out of the chair to answer the call of duty. 'I'll just . . . I'll have to . . .'

'It's all right,' Betty said. 'I'll do it.'

'Would you?' Gemma drained her glass and held it out abstractedly, seeming not to notice that the professor was leaping to refill it. 'Oh, but . . .'

'Are you sure?' Freddie was unable to conceal her relief that someone else was volunteering.

'Don't worry,' Betty said grimly. 'It's only going to be once around the block — and I won't cross any streets. If they don't like it — too bad.'

'Good for you!' Professor Borley said. It was the first sign of rebellion that Betty had shown since the reception.

'Well . . .' Gemma's relief was palpable. 'If you really don't mind, dear. You know where I keep their leashes . . .' She lowered the liquid level in her glass. 'So very kind of you . . . all of you. . . .'

Abby Borley was at her elbow, topping up the depleted glass. He seemed to have decided that, if there was only one thing he could do to help, he was going to do that thing thoroughly.

'Take care!' Freddie said, as Betty went for the dogs. 'Even just around the block. We don't want —' She broke off, not even wanting to voice what they didn't want.

'Oh, dear . . .' Gemma hiccuped. 'Life was so simple . . . so pleasant . . . when we first moved here. What happened? What went wrong?'

The pugs surged into the room, frisking

around it, exploring the small dishes of nuts and Twiglets, sniffing at the guests, and then converged on Gemma, nearly knocking the glass out of her hand.

'There now . . . there now.' Gemma tried to calm them. 'It's all right . . . Betty's going to take you walkies.'

Betty came back into the room with their leashes, but they were jumping around too much for her to affix them to their collars. Gemma took over and hitched them up deftly.

'We won't be long,' Betty said, tugging at the leashes.

'Don't take them down Coffers Passage!' Lorinda was suddenly assailed by the memory of how sinister that alleyway had become to her, especially at night when it was dark and deserted.

'I wasn't planning to.' Betty gave her an odd look as the dogs impatiently pulled her through the doorway.

'Be careful, dear,' Gemma called after her. 'Don't let them knock you off your feet.'

'Betty is stronger than she looks,' the professor said. 'You don't have to worry about her.'

'She has to be, to cope with Dorian, never mind the rest of us.' Freddie absently accepted a refill and sipped at it.

'It's the dogs —' How silly they had been to think that Gemma might have been worried about Betty. 'If they get away from her, they'll run wild. They . . . they could be . . . run over. Oh! I never should have let Opal take them out last night! I wasn't that ill. I should have walked them myself.'

'Water under the bridge now. Nothing we can do to change it. And,' Abby Borley added clumsily, 'if you had, it might have been you who died.'

'No.' Gemma was firm on that point. 'No, I wouldn't have taken the dogs in that direction. I wouldn't have been in the wrong place at that wrong time.'

'You can't tell for certain.' He tried to retrieve his tactlessness. 'Maybe she intended to go another way, but changed her mind. I guess you just have to figure that it was Appointment In Samarra time for her.'

'Oh, but —' Gemma hiccuped abruptly. 'Sorry.' She gave a sudden wild giggle and hiccuped again. 'Oh, dear!'

They looked at each other and then at the cocktail shaker Abby was still holding.

'You're exhausted,' Freddie said tactfully. 'And this has been a nasty shock. Why don't you lie down for a while?'

'No, no, I'm quite all — hic! — right. I

must take care of the dogs, they'll be back soon.'

'Betty can see to them, she's done it before.' Freddie gently urged Gemma to her feet. 'Come along now, you'll feel a lot better after a little rest.'

'If you think so.' Gemma swayed. 'Oh, but I must lock the door and —'

'Don't worry about anything,' Abby said. 'We'll take care of all that.'

'So kind . . . so very kind . . .' She allowed Freddie to lead her from the room.

'Sad.' Abby watched them go, shaking his head. 'Very sad, but it isn't as though she'd been lifelong buddies with that cousin. It's mostly shock. And maybe we'll get a bit of peace around here now.'

'Gemma did say something about disturbed nights,' Lorinda remembered. 'She didn't go into details, though. I gather her cousin could be rather trying.'

'Not so much Opal as the other one.' He sank into an armchair and stretched out his long legs, crossing them at the ankle, prepared for a gossip. 'Although, if Opal hadn't been here, there wouldn't have been a problem.'

'Oh . . . ?' Lorinda encouraged.

'I probably shouldn't be telling you this.' He leaned forward. Try to stop him. 'But

. . . it has been hell around here since Dorian brought that other woman home. Opal on her own was all right — and, I'm sure, Adèle on her own would have been all right. But the two of them in close proximity . . .' He shook his head.

'It's because they have the same series character,' Lorinda said. 'If they were working on different series, they might even have become friends. As it is — was . . .'

'Two dogs fighting over a bone,' he agreed. 'Which I wouldn't mind, if they hadn't disrupted everyone around them in their battles.'

'Gemma said something about doors slamming in the night . . .' Lorinda prodded.

'That was the least of it,' he sighed. 'So childish — nasty notes pushed under the door in the middle of the night. Nuisance telephone calls with a hang-up when the phone was answered. Gemma had to unplug the telephone, but she couldn't do much about the doorbell. And poor Betty has been badgered just about out of her mind by the two of them, demanding to get a look at each other's chapters —'

A clamour at the front door announced that poor put-upon Betty had concluded another of her tasks and returned with the dogs. There was a clatter in the front hall as they were released from their leashes and they bounded into the living room, looking for their mistress.

'She went thataway.' Abby pointed and the pugs took off for the bedroom. He stood and had a drink ready to thrust into Betty's hand when she came into the room and slumped into an armchair.

'Thank you.' She smiled weakly. 'I need that.'

'It seems so excessive,' Lorinda was still musing. 'They've each carved out their own niche and seem to be doing well. I mean, why bother with a harassment campaign?'

'I was just telling Lorinda about some of the problems we've been having here,' Abby explained in answer to Betty's enquiring look.

'Professional jealousy,' she said crisply. 'They were both sick with it.'

'It's something deeper than that,' Abby said. 'I've seen it in the academic world, especially among biographers. First, they think they own the character, then they begin to think they *are* the character. And, if two of them find out they're working on the same subject — well! Hell truly hath no fury like that of an outraged archivist. There were times when I wouldn't have been surprised to have seen murder done.'

'You think that's what happened here?' Freddie paused in the doorway as the unpleasant word seemed to echo through the room. 'Again?'

'Strange . . .' Betty emptied her glass and set it down, shaking her head as Abby proffered a refill. 'I had a mental bet on it happening the other way around. I was sure that Opal was going to be the one to dispose of Adèle. After all, she's been here longer and knows the territory. I thought she had the advantage.'

'An automobile is as great a leveller as a gun,' Abby said. 'With the added advantage of an element of doubt. A car accident always could have been an accident. It's harder to pass it off as an accident when someone is blasted with a bullet.'

' "*I didn't know the gun was loaded*",' Freddie could not resist singing.

'And let's hope she never, ever does it again,' Abby agreed. 'Mind you, she has no reason to now. Opal was her *bête noire*.'

'We don't know that Adèle actually did anything.' Lorinda was beginning to feel sorry for the woman. Even Dorian thought she was to blame, and now the others were making a case against her. 'Whatever happened to "innocent until proven guilty"?'

'Frankly, my dears . . .' Abby Borley yawned and stretched. 'I don't give a damn which one of them killed the other, just so long as we now get a bit of peace around here!'

Chapter Sixteen

They were talking about him again. He wasn't being paranoid, he knew it.

Detective Chief Superintendent Derringdo pulled his hand away from the fresh scab on his chin. Mustn't pick it. He had enough scars. Enough worries.

He wished he could stop worrying and just concentrate on his job, but how could he? The doctor had just rung to tell him the tests had confirmed the diagnosis: the five-year-old twins had leukaemia — both of them.

And young Lesley, nearly seven, was due for her hole-in-the-heart operation next week.

'Tea, guv'nor?' WPC Bentley hovered over him worshipfully. She had been like that ever since he had rescued her from the mad axeman who'd been holding her hostage. 'Or coffee? Can I get you a sandwich? It's chicken curry in the staff can-

teen today — I could bring you some.'

'Just coffee, thanks.' Why did women always want to feed you? Especially when they were invariably on a diet themselves. His older sister, Angie, was a case in point. Been on a diet all her life, down to about six stone now. Sometimes he wondered: could it be anorexia? Rum, that.

Rum, yes. And vodka. Never mind the coffee, that was what he wanted: a whole bottle of vodka, followed by rum, scotch, beer, brandy . . . He'd been on the wagon for twelve whole hours now. God, it was hard! Agony! Perhaps he'd let himself have just a snifter or two tonight when he got home.

But first he would have to stop by the Special Needs school on the way home and pick up little Simon, the eight-year-old. If it was a good day, Simon might even speak to him.

'Sir —' Detective Sergeant Croxley was beside the desk, holding a sheaf of computer printouts. 'Sir, we've got him! That villain you pulled in last night. He's Mr Big! We've found his warehouse — it's crammed to the gunnels with firearms, ammunition and a whole mountain of drugs. We've got him dead to rights!'

'Oh. Er, good. Good work, lad.' He hoped his young and enthusiastic team attributed his bleak croak to the fact that he was concerned because his mother was not recovering properly from her hip replacement operation and it might have to be done again.

How long could he keep it from them that his baby sister had eloped with Mr Big six weeks ago? She had even made it legal — they were married. And how was he going to break it to Cissy that her bridegroom would be going down for a very long stretch?

Oh, yes — and under the new regulations, Mr Big's house, chattels and bank accounts would be seized. Cissy would not take kindly to being made a pauper. . . .

At the end of a long day, his home looked almost welcoming as he approached it. But he was not deceived.

He carried Simon up the stairs, the child's leg brace hitting against his sore ribs with every step.

Tomorrow, he promised himself, tomorrow he would try to put aside his personal problems and concentrate on solving the murder of the elderly much-loved local vicar. The tabloids were already baying at his heels about it and he was afraid that his job was on the line. Again.

At the top of the stairs, he set Simon down on the floor and gave him an encouraging pat on the shoulder.

'Run along now,' he said absently.

'Run? Run? You fool!' Christine, his wife, appeared out of the shadows. In a raging temper, as usual. 'Hobble, you mean! You know he can't run! He'll never run! Hobble, hobble along, Simon, like a good little cripple!'

'Christine!' He tried to be understanding, to empathize with her. 'I'm sorry. The doctor rang me about the twins this afternoon. Don't worry, we'll get through it somehow —'

'The twins! Simon! Lesley! There's something wrong with every one of your children! Your genes are rotten! Useless! Damned —'

'Oh, really?' He tried to keep calm and rational. 'Has it ever occurred to you that it might be your —'

That was as far as he got. Where had that heavy iron frying pan come from? She must have been hiding it behind her skirt.

'No! Don't!' he shouted, raising his arms to shield his head.

'Shut up! Shut up!' She lashed out with the frying pan. 'Do you want the neighbours to hear you?'

No! No! That must never happen! *He lowered his arms and grappled with her, trying to get control of the makeshift weapon.*

She kicked out and he felt his knees give way. He crashed heavily down the stairs, trying again to shield his face to minimize any visible bruising that would betray his shame to the world. The floor rose up to meet him. He clenched his teeth to keep from crying out.

No one must ever know. To his dying breath, he must guard the worst, the most shameful, secret of all:

That he, the brilliant detective, the hero of a hundred daring raids, the re-spected Detective Chief Superintendent, the man with hopes of becoming Chief Constable some day . . . that he . . . of all people . . . was a battered husband.

The cats no longer even blinked when a paperback went soaring over their heads. To be honest, she hadn't thrown it with her customary vigour. The storyline had brought back the sudden disturbing memory of the bruises on Macho's face the other week. Those bruises had faded away now and no fresh ones had appeared.

Did that mean that Cressie was growing better at controlling her temper — possibly because she was getting her own way? Or did it mean that she was striking where the bruises wouldn't show?

What's it to you? The echo from that earlier unsettling dream returned to her, so vividly that it was hard to remember that it had been just a dream . . . a nightmare . . .

What *was* it to her?

Macho Magee was a colleague, a neighbour, an old friend who had grown more endearing since they had moved into nearby houses in this comfortable retreat. Macho Magee — No! — Lancelot Dalrymple was a sweet gentle man and a scholar, a man who deserved better in life than a termagant . . . a domineering shrew . . . a . . . a Cressie! Why couldn't he come to his senses and realize that?

What was it to *her?*

She caught up as many of the remaining paperbacks as she could hold in each hand and hurled them across the room, this time with considerable force.

The cats went skittering for the exit, colliding with each other in their eagerness to get out of her way.

She continued throwing until there were no books left. Then, for good measure, she crossed the room and kicked them into an untidy heap. There! They could stay there! She wouldn't waste another moment on them, far less force herself to read them. Perhaps tomorrow, she'd gather them up and hand them over to Freddie —

Freddie! She was supposed to be at Freddie's for dinner! Tonight . . . now! She was late — and she still had to change into something more suitable for a social evening.

Had-I and But-Known raced inside the moment Freddie opened the door. Sniffing rapturously, they made straight for the kitchen, following the heady aroma of roasting chicken.

'Can you take them anywhere?' Lorinda shrugged an apology.

'Funny, I got the impression they were taking you. I do admit, however, that you have better manners. Come in.'

'Are we the first to arrive?' Lorinda admired the inviting scene: bowls of nibbles on the tables, along with vases of spring blooms. Soft music played in the background.

'You've really pushed the boat out.'

'I thought I'd remind Macho what civilized living is like,' Freddie said. 'I don't have the feeling that he sees much of it with Cressie.'

A sudden loud crash from the other half of the semi-detached made them both jump.

'That is,' Freddie added bitterly, 'if my dear neighbours can restrain themselves. Otherwise, Macho will think he's still in the War Zone.'

'So the Jackleys *are* back. I know Dorian had that postcard from Karla saying that they were on their way, but I haven't seen them around.'

'Neither have I, but for the past few days I've been hearing the occasional thump and bump on the other side of the wall. I assume they're back, although some of the old fire seems to be missing. Perhaps they aren't well.'

'Or perhaps they have deadlines to meet before they can allow themselves to get back in the social swim.'

'Anyway,' Freddie sighed, 'the peace and quiet was great — while it lasted. And, so long as I don't admit that I've noticed that they're back, I don't have to do anything about it.'

'Good thinking.' Lorinda was in perfect accord, she didn't want to have to start coping with the Jackleys again, either. Cressie was quite enough to be going on with.

Following immediately upon that thought, the doorbell rang. The temperature of the room dropped by about fifteen degrees when Freddie ushered them in. It was easy to see why.

Macho held Roscoe clasped to his chest and Cressie was in an icy fury about it. Freddie and Lorinda exchanged glances; they would be lucky if the next heavy thuds didn't come from this side of the wall.

'Hello, Roscoe,' Freddie said: he seemed to be the safest member of the trio to speak to. 'Nice to see you again.' Casually, she removed a heavy crystal ashtray that now did duty as an almond dish from within too-easy reach, replacing it with a plastic dish full of cashews.

Roscoe miaowed a polite rejoinder and Cressie made a barely repressed sound of disgust.

'And you, too, of course, Cressie,' Freddie said. 'And Macho.'

Macho nodded glumly, neither looking at the others nor releasing his hold on Roscoe, who was beginning to squirm restlessly as he scented the chicken.

Had-I and But-Known appeared in the doorway, lured from the kitchen by the sound of Roscoe's voice.

'God!' Cressie exploded. 'I don't believe you people! You even take your damned animals with you when you go out to dinner!'

'They're welcome guests, too,' Freddie said mildly. 'If I'm not complaining, I don't see why you should.'

'Go and join your friends.' Macho let Roscoe slip to the floor. Had-I and But-Known came forward to meet him, touching noses before leading him off to the kitchen.

'And don't think you're breaking your diet!' Cressie shouted after him viciously.

Macho's eyes narrowed, but he didn't say anything. *We'll see about that!* hung in the air.

'Drinks!' Freddie intervened briskly, trying to avert the threatened scene. 'Dry sherry . . .' She began to pour. '*Very* dry sherry, in view of the menu.'

'I don't like sherry,' Cressie said flatly. 'Don't you have any vodka?'

'Sorry,' Freddie said, 'I used up all the vodka in the first course.'

'You did?' Lorinda felt a faint stir of

alarm. 'What are we having?'

'I told you it was an experiment,' Freddie said.

'That's where the vodka went?' Bemused and forgetting her earlier declaration, Cressie accepted her sherry and sipped it absently. 'What kind of experiment?'

'Wait and see.' Freddie raised her glass. 'Cheers!'

'Cheers!' Macho responded, lifting his glass with a barely veiled sneer at Cressie for starting before the toast.

Someone's been feeding him meat! Lorinda thought. *And I'll bet it wasn't Cressie!*

'Anyway,' Freddie smiled at Cressie, trying to defuse the situation, 'isn't it lucky that you haven't sent your party invitations out?'

'What do you mean?'

'It saves you the bother of having to cancel them.'

'Cancel? Why should I want to cancel the party?'

'Because you can't have it now.' It should have been obvious. 'All things considered.'

'What things?' Cressie glared at her. 'It's going to be the most exciting party this place has ever seen. Everyone has heard about it and is looking forward to it.

Everyone I talk to has been hinting for an invitation. Nothing has changed.'

'Nothing?' Freddie asked unbelievingly, looking towards Macho, who was oblivious. 'Most people would consider a death in the family a good enough reason to put festivities on hold.'

'It's not my family,' Cressie said.

'Look.' Freddie spelled it out. 'You cannot hold a big party in a house where one of the occupants has just died. For heaven's sake, they haven't even done the autopsy yet.'

'Autopsy?' Cressie looked shaken. 'Why should they want to do that?'

'It's customary,' Lorinda joined the fray, 'in the case of a sudden unexplained death.'

'What do you mean, unexplained? She was hit by a car.'

'The second person to be struck by a car,' Macho was paying attention, after all, 'in as many months. The police will have noticed that. They'll want measurements, noting locations of breaks and bruises, to try to ascertain if the same car was involved both times.'

'You people!' Cressie distanced herself from them, shuddering. 'How could it be the same car? Adèle Desparta hadn't hit town yet when the first accident happened.'

There it was again. That cool certainty that Adèle had disposed of her rival. And no one had even heard — or cared about — her side of the story. This town was turning into one big hanging jury — it was just as well that the death penalty had been abolished. Even so, fifteen to twenty years in jail wouldn't do Adèle Desparta any good.

'Has it ever occurred to you —' Lorinda began.

'That's it!' Freddie drained her glass and made shooing motions towards the kitchen. 'Let's get started. Quick before it melts!'

Since it was still in the freezer, there was little chance of that. Freddie took out a bowl, fluffed up the contents with a fork, divided them into sherbert glasses and sloshed a bit more vodka over the tops.

'Here we are,' she said. 'You've heard of the Bloody Mary, you've heard of the Virgin Mary. Now we present — *taa-daah!* — the Frigid Mary!'

'What is it?' Cressie looked at the frosted red mass with suspicion.

'Try it and see,' Freddie said.

'It's a frozen Bloody Mary.' Macho had

already dipped into his. 'Were you expecting real blood?'

'With you people, who can tell?' Cressie poked at it moodily.

Lorinda and Freddie exchanged glances. It was clear that whatever bloom had once been on the rose had now definitely vanished. But, if Cressie was so miserable here, why did she stay? She had her own place in London, hadn't she? That vaunted mews house, whose renovation she had so exhaustively and harrowingly detailed in *Mooning the Builders*.

'This tastes funny.' Cressie was determined not to be satisfied. For an instant, Lorinda felt a fleeting sympathy for the builders.

'Everyone has their own recipe for a Bloody Mary.' Macho eyed her coldly. 'This is Freddie's. It tastes just fine to me.'

'You all stick together,' Cressie complained.

No one bothered to answer. Lorinda watched as Freddie crossed to the oven, stalked by the cats.

'Now for the pièce de résistance — I hope!' Freddie lifted a pan from the oven and swiftly transferred the golden chicken to a platter and placed it in the centre of the table.

'Well, it's golden in patches.' She eyed her handiwork judiciously. 'Could be worse. It's probably the sort of thing that needs a bit more practice.'

'What have you done to it?' Cressie asked.

'Gilded it,' Freddie said. 'Or, as it was known in medieval times, "endored" it.'

'Medieval, eh?' Macho studied the bird with interest. 'From one of your old recipe books, no doubt.'

'No, I mean, why is it so flat? Did you hit it with a rolling pin?' Cressie wrinkled her nose. 'It looks like a shelf between the two wings. Is that medieval, too?'

'No, that's modern — I think.' It seemed that Cressie had hit a sensitive spot. 'All the current advice is to roast your chicken breast down for the first half-hour, then turn it over on its back for the rest of the cooking time, and it gives you lots of moist juicy breast meat. So I tried it — and this is what happened. That damned bird went into the oven a 36C and when I turned it over, it was a 32A. I hoped it might plump up again when I put it back in the oven, but it didn't.'

'Your medieval cook would have cooked it on a spit.' Macho seemed to be having trouble controlling his expression. 'It would eliminate that problem.'

'It probably tastes all right,' Lorinda said, 'even if it does look a bit peculiar.'

'I hope you're right.' Having allowed them enough time to contemplate it, Freddie began to carve briskly. 'Let's see how it tastes.'

'I don't like it.' Predictably, Cressie balked at the first forkful. 'It tastes weird.'

'That's probably the saffron,' Freddie said. 'It's not everybody's cup of tea — but it enhances the gold colour.'

'Medieval food was usually highly flavoured.' Macho spoke with authority. 'And often too strong or too sweet to appeal to modern tastes. On the whole,' he chewed reflectively, 'this isn't too bad, but I think I prefer your usual way of roasting it, right side up and covered with strips of bacon.'

The cats circled the table, alert for kindness or carelessness. Lorinda let a small chunk of chicken slip to the floor as Roscoe nudged her ankle.

Had-I and But-Known promptly crowded over, demanding their share — and giving her away.

'Are you feeding that cat?' Cressie glared at her.

'Not really,' Lorinda defended. 'It just fell off my fork.'

'Put that cat out!' Cressie ordered Macho. 'Put them all out! They shouldn't be in here when people are eating, anyway. It's unsanitary!'

'No!' Macho said.

'What???'

'You heard me!'

'Nevertheless, I believe I'll put this recipe in the book.' Freddie's voice over-rode the others. 'It's simple enough — and an experienced cook might be able to adjust the recipe enough to get better results.'

'It's a sort of sauce, is it?' Lorinda tried to keep up her end of the conversation. 'That should be easy.'

'It looked easy,' Freddie sighed. 'Just one ounce of butter, a quarter teaspoon of saffron, an ounce of sugar, two tablespoons of white wine vinegar and one egg yolk. Bob's your uncle, I thought — until I started cooking it. But when I melted the butter and all the salty scum rose to the surface, I realized that they should have specified un-salted butter. Then you're supposed to stir in the saffron and cook it gently until the butter turns bright yellow — only the butter started to brown and it was a race to get the colour out of the saffron strands before the butter burned black. When it came to straining out the saffron, I didn't want to clog up my tea strainer with congealing butter, so I used a fork — it was like fishing spider legs out of the lemonade on a summer picnic.'

There was a gagging sound from Cressie.

'Then you add the sugar and wine vinegar to the saffroned butter and cook it until it goes syrupy, when you take it off the heat and stir in the egg yolk and cook, but don't boil, stirring constantly, until it's thick — only it started going lumpy. I think they should have told you to use a double-boiler, otherwise it cooks too fast. Then you slosh the gloop over your chicken and put the bird back in the oven for the last ten minutes or so to finish cooking.' Freddie regarded the results gloomily. 'I'm not sure it was worth it.'

'Oh, I don't know. I may try that,' Lorinda said unconvincingly, privately thinking that, in these modern times, it might be easier just to rub some yellow food colouring over the chicken.

'It could have a certain novelty value for special festivities,' Freddie said. 'But I've also decided that — just to give the readers a break — it would be more merciful to include some recipes from the past that no one in their right mind would want to try.

It would make such a nice change for them to just sit and read without feeling that they ought to be getting up and going to the kitchen to try out the recipe.'

'Have you anything particular in mind?' Lorinda's voice rang out too loudly, now that the others had lapsed into silence. Cressie was sulking as Macho defiantly picked up a generous slice of chicken and hand-fed it to Roscoe. The brooding hunch of her shoulders told them all that he was going to regret that the instant she got him alone.

For the moment, with his peers around him, he was safe. And so was Roscoe. Freddie heaped more slices of chicken on to Macho's plate.

'As a matter of fact, I have. Artificial Ass's Milk,' Freddie said. 'I found it in an eighteenth-century cookery book.'

'What the hell do you do with ass's milk?' Cressie's attention was diverted.

'Cleopatra bathed in it,' Macho told her.

'This one is supposed to be a drink for invalids,' Freddie said, 'but I think you'd rather bathe in it than drink it.'

'Maybe I would.' Cressie pointedly scraped the gilding off another piece of chicken.

'It also minimizes any guilt feelings because you not only can't get the ingredients these days, you've never heard of most of them. For instance, hartshorn shavings, eringo root, China root, balsam of Tolu — but the zinger is: "eighteen snails bruised with the shells" . . .'

'Correction,' Cressie said. 'I don't even want to bathe in it.'

'How do you bruise a snail?' Macho wondered.

'After that, it gets pretty tame,' Freddie said. 'You're supposed to boil it all up with real milk. Then the invalid is supposed to drink half a pint in the morning and half a pint at night.'

'And it didn't kill them?' Cressie's eyes were wide.

'Our ancestors were a hardy lot,' Macho said. 'They had to be, what with the leeches and blood-letting and all. Not to mention the amateur herbalists who got it wrong.'

There was a sudden loud crash from the other half of the house.

'The Jackleys are back, are they?' Macho looked towards the wall. 'I haven't seen them around the village.'

'Nor have I.' Freddie shrugged. 'They must be lying low for some reason.'

'You mean you don't really know who

you've got living next door?' Cressie seemed apprehensive.

'Jack and Karla are,' Freddie said.

'But, if you haven't actually seen them, it could be anyone. They might have sublet. You're awfully trusting. There are a lot of strange people around these days.'

'You're not in the city now. We all know our neighbours here. We may not like them very much —' Freddie glared at the wall as another muffled thump shook it — 'but we know who they are.'

'Stop that!' Cressie bellowed suddenly. Roscoe had crept into Macho's lap and was eating the chicken at the side of his plate.

'You knew he was doing that!' She turned her fury on Macho. 'You were letting him do it!'

Macho gave her a cold stare and deliberately hand-fed Roscoe another choice sliver.

'That does it! If you don't throw him out, I will!' She charged around the table and snatched Roscoe from Macho's lap. Roscoe protested violently, twisting in her grasp and clawing out.

Had-I went over to investigate and unwisely stepped into her path. Cressie lashed out with her foot.

The shrieks came simultaneously: Lorinda's, as she rushed from the table to rescue Had-I; Cressie's, as a claw caught in her forearm and raked it, leaving a long scratch that began welling blood.

Roscoe dropped to the floor and raced into the living room. Had-I, shocked and bewildered, nestled into Lorinda's arms — no one had ever treated her like that before.

'I'm bleeding!' Cressie shrieked.

'Bleeding nuisance!' Macho muttered, not quite under his breath.

'Here, sit down.' Freddie pushed a chair towards her. 'I'll fix it. It's just a scratch.'

'No, you don't! You'd probably poison me with one of those old recipes of yours!! You're crazy!' Cressie wrenched open the back door and darted for home. 'You're all crazy!'

In the silence, Freddie returned to her place at the table, sat down and buried her face in her hands. Her voice was muffled: 'There's nothing like a nice quiet dinner with friends.'

'I'm sorry,' Macho apologized. 'She's upset.'

'*I'm* sorry, but that's just not good enough!' Lorinda was still furious. 'That woman is a menace. You've got to get rid of her before — before she kills all our cats!'

'She wouldn't do that. Well, she would, if she could,' Macho admitted. 'But I won't let her.'

'You haven't done a very good job so far,' Lorinda said. 'Poor Roscoe is —'

'I know, I know.' He rubbed his forehead.

'Macho . . .' Freddie raised her head and stared into his eyes. 'This has gone too far. Let's have the truth: are you married to that woman?'

'God, no!' Macho shuddered.

'Then why don't you get rid of her? What hold does she have over you?'

There was a long silence.

'Macho . . . ?' Lorinda asked.

'Oh, all right.' He caved in. 'I guess the project is well enough along now to tell you. We . . . we're collaborating on a new book. Something different for both of us.'

'How different?' They waited.

'We're using my knowledge of history and her, er, cutting edge and we're writing *Anne Boleyn Is Missing!*' He sat back and looked at them with a faint air of triumph — and some relief.

'You mean you're writing alternative history?' Lorinda was dubious. 'Like, Anne

Boleyn went missing before she got involved with Henry VIII?'

'No, no, it's completely modern. Up-to-date.' Macho drew a deep breath. 'The concept is: Someone is Stealing the Stately Ghosts of England. One by one, they're all disappearing from their, er, accustomed haunts, the stately homes and historic sites.'

'You mean someone is spiriting away the spirits?'

'If you want to put it like that.' Macho did not appreciate Freddie's levity. 'I'm providing the solid historical background and Cressie is doing all the, um, sex scenes.'

There was another long silence.

'Sex . . . with ghosts . . . ?' Freddie got a faraway look in her eyes. 'But —'

'Oh, get your mind out of the gutter!' Macho snapped.

'The ectoplasm, actually,' Freddie drawled.

The telephone began to ring. 'That will be Cressie.' Macho flinched. 'I ought to be going. Where's Roscoe?'

'Why don't you let me take care of him tonight?' Lorinda suggested. 'I think it might be . . . better.'

'Yes, yes, you're right. She's in a filthy

mood — and he did scratch her. If it's not too much trouble, I'd be most grateful.'

'No trouble at all,' Lorinda assured him truthfully. Roscoe had often been an overnight guest . . . before Cressie.

'You could always pack that book in.' Freddie tried again. 'And then you could send her packing.'

'No, I couldn't.' Macho moved abjectly towards the door, as the telephone continued ringing. 'You don't understand.'

'But —'

'It's too late. We've already got a six-figure advance from New York for it!'

Chapter Seventeen

'No!' Lorinda looked down in horror at the offering at her feet. 'Oh, no! You didn't! Tell me you didn't!'

But-Known looked up at her brightly. If she were a dog, she would have wagged her tail. She was proud of herself — just look what she'd brought home.

'No, no, no!' Lorinda closed her eyes but, when she opened them again, the offering hadn't gone away.

A weather-beaten, bedraggled, miniature teddy bear still lay at her feet.

'Tell me you didn't raid the shrine,' she said hopelessly, knowing it was the only explanation. '*Please,* tell me you didn't.'

'*Prrrymmph,*' But-Known said proudly. This was the most interesting thing she had found in ages — and far nicer than the blood-leaking mice and birds Had-I brought home. She waited expectantly for the praise that was her due.

'Yes, darling, yes, yes.' Lorinda bent to bestow the expected caresses. 'Good girl, clever girl. You weren't to know. Oh, heavens, what am I to do?'

Nothing until darkness had fallen, obviously. Then she'd have to try to put it back, hoping no one had noticed it was missing. And that was another worry: had anyone seen But-Known dragging her booty home?

Had-I strolled past and glanced disparagingly at her sister's offering. Not even edible! Her look promised Lorinda something much juicier as soon as *she* had a chance to go hunting.

'Don't bother,' Lorinda told her. '*Please* don't bother.'

Dampness was in the air and a rising wind was sending clouds scudding across the face of the quarter-moon when Lorinda opened her front door and surveyed the territory before venturing outside.

The coast seemed to be clear. She had carefully waited until Gemma had finished walking her dogs, which usually marked the end of the evening's activities along the High Street.

She was alone as she reached the shrine. Automatically, she glanced around before

249

taking the little teddy bear from her rain-coat pocket. From past experience, she would not have been surprised to find Betty Alvin lurking nearby.

The light from the lamp illuminated the sad offerings tied to the post. She tried to spot the place from which But-Known had removed her bloodless prey. If she put it back in the wrong position, the person who had originally tied it into place might notice. Or was Betty the only person still paying close attention to the shrine? And why was she so concerned about it?

For that matter, why was Betty always on foot these days? What had happened to the rather rattly little car she usually drove about in?

Lorinda frowned as the implications of that thought struck her. Betty? Never! No, it wouldn't do to start suspecting one of the most useful members of their little community. What would any of them do without Betty? Good secretarial services were not otherwise available in this area.

And yet . . . it was worth remembering that Adèle was not the only person who might have hated Opal. From what Professor Borley had said, both Opal and Adèle had harassed poor Betty almost to the point of a nervous breakdown. And

Opal had been living in the same building, with far more opportunity to waylay Betty and attempt to suborn her. Backed up by Gemma, of course. It would not be altogether surprising if Betty, nerve-racked and exhausted, had seen Opal with the dogs and given way to a deadly impulse, or perhaps she only meant to frighten her.

Only . . . it was the child's shrine Betty was haunting. Surely, Betty couldn't have been responsible for that. Yet most of the same conditions applied: exhausted, harassed, badgered, rehearsing her grievances as she drove along . . . a moment's inattention . . . and then the panic and instinctive rush to escape. It was possible . . . it was only too possible . . .

Lorinda was stooping to replace the teddy bear in what she hoped was the correct spot when she heard the roar of a motor. She looked up to see a car bearing down on her, seeming to aim itself straight at her.

Caught between the car and the lamp post, she threw herself to one side and went sprawling.

Brakes screamed and a car door slammed. Dazed, Lorinda lay still, unwilling — she hoped not unable — to move.

'Are you all right?' Adèle Desparta held

out a hand to help her up. 'What on earth did you do that for?'

'I tripped,' Lorinda said, feeling silly.

'You panicked,' Adèle corrected. 'Has Dorian been spreading tales of my dangerous driving?'

'Not at all.' What was it Dorian had said? Front right bumper. Lorinda tried to take an unobtrusive look. Sure enough, there was a large dent in it.

'Dorian's a fool!' Adèle snapped. 'Oh, I know what he's been saying. He couldn't resist letting me know that he knew my "guilty secret". And, in view of the way Dorian operates, I'm probably the *last* to know! That damned bumper was dented when I picked up the car! I was furious about it, but it was the only car available and I needed one immediately.'

'Umm . . .' Lorinda could not think of a suitable response, not that Adèle gave her time enough.

'And now I can't use it! I wanted to go up to Derbyshire, to Hardwick Hall, just to walk around it again and absorb the atmosphere. Now I can't leave this stinking village — or everyone will think I'm running away!'

'Oh, surely not,' Lorinda murmured.

'No?' Adèle strode back to the car,

pulling Lorinda with her, and opened the door to the passenger seat. 'Get in!'

'Er . . .' Lorinda held back. It was one thing to be willing to give Adèle the benefit of the doubt but . . . to the extent of getting into the car with her and driving off into the unknown? Especially when there was no one to witness her departure?

'You see?' Adèle said grimly.

'No, really, it's not that,' Lorinda protested. 'It's just that I have to feed the cats before . . .'

'Before what?' Adèle challenged. 'Before you let me kill you?'

'I didn't say that!'

'You didn't have to. It's what you're thinking. It's what everybody in town is thinking!'

Lorinda could not deny it, but she tried frantically to do so. 'Oh, not —'

'Not everybody? Oh, no? And they're all such fools! Opal's death was the last thing I wanted! Do you know what's happening now?' Adèle was working herself into a monumental fury. 'Back in the States, they think *I'm* the one who died! The news reports of Opal's death just identified her as "the author of the popular Bess of Hardwick series". My series is much better known than hers — and the stupid moronic bastards think it's *me!*'

'Oh, dear. I know a lot of the fans identify us with — and by — our characters, but that's a bit much!' (How many times had people referred to her as Miss Petunia on her tour? And enquired earnestly as to the health of Lily and Marigold? It had been quite disconcerting at times. Downright creepy at other times.)

'You work your butt off to get published,' Adèle continued bitterly. 'You get a fan base and begin to think you're established — and then you discover that nine out of ten of the stupid semi-literate bastards don't even know your name. And the tenth thinks you're dead already!'

'It can't be that bad.'

'Can't it? They're posting tributes on *DorothyL*. We've just stopped an obit being run in *Publishers Weekly*. And even my publishers have been on to my agent to ask where they should send flowers. With some of the covers I've had over the years,' she added, with increasing bitterness, 'I always knew the Art Department couldn't read, but I did hold higher hopes for Editorial.'

'I know just what you mean.' Lorinda nodded glumly. 'Only three books ago, my —'

'Oh!' Lorinda turned to find that the startled voice belonged to Hilda Saint. 'Good evening. I didn't expect to see anyone else out at this hour.'

'It's only eleven thirty.' From the way Adèle looked at her, she might have arrived from a different planet.

'Yes, I know. But we're "early to bed, early to rise" people around here. Usually.'

'Adèle, you've met Hilda Saint, haven't you?' Lorinda said quickly. 'She has the best guest house in town.'

'But you're Dorian's guest, aren't you?' Hilda's tone was chilly, giving the distinct impression of bread having been snatched from her mouth.

'Naturally. We're old friends,' Adèle said, with equal chill.

'So I understand.' Hilda's gaze slid over the front bumper, not quite surreptitiously enough.

'It was like that when I collected it!' Adèle ground out between clenched teeth.

'Oh, yes, I'm sure it was.' Hilda smiled falsely. 'So unreliable, some of these car hire firms.'

'And what are you doing out and about at this hour, Hilda?' Lorinda reversed the attack. 'I thought you'd be in bed and asleep by now.'

'Ordinarily, I would be.' Hilda sighed deeply. 'But, when one has the builders in, one's life isn't one's own. I'm almost sorry I started the extension now. An extension seemed like a simple project when I first thought of it, but the complications . . .'

'You should compare notes with Cressie.'

'Yes, I know. I've read her book. It's made my experience seem like a case of déjà vu — right down to the nasty little notes slipped under my bedroom door to tell me how much the price of something has gone up, because he hasn't the nerve to tell me face to face.'

'Ripping you off, are they?' Lorinda sympathized.

'To say the least of it, but what can you do? It seems they're all alike. Although I must say the pressure has eased *slightly* since they've found themselves a place to stay down here. At least they show up earlier.'

'They're not staying at your place?'

'Never! I know enough not to mix business with business. Which is more than they do. I'm *sure* they're sneaking off to work at the new housing development on the other side of the hill when they disappear for hours at a time during the day.'

'Perhaps Cressie could give you a few

hints about handling them —'

'You obviously never read her book! She was battling with hers constantly and, every time she complained, they did something terrible to the foundations or the utilities. Mind you, reading between the lines, I think there was more going on between her and the head builder than she was admitting. A degree of personal spite seemed to be involved. And, of course, I don't really think mine would act like that but —'

'But you wouldn't put it past them,' Adèle finished for her.

'Well, possibly not.' Hilda shifted uneasily and moved a little farther away, obviously uncomfortable to find herself agreeing with Adèle about anything.

Adèle smiled nastily and deliberately moved closer. She had noticed Hilda's instinctive withdrawal, which was now repeated, as was Adèle's advance. Lorinda watched bemused as the two women edged their way around the lamp post in a complete circle, winding up where they had begun. Hilda was beginning to develop a nervous twitch at the corner of her mouth.

It might have been laughable, were it not for the fact that Hilda was illustrating all too clearly the attitude of the villagers towards Adèle. It was so much more comfortable to believe that a stranger was responsible than to think that one of them might have done it. A newcomer, a stranger and a foreigner — Adèle fitted the requirements perfectly. And her own attitude wasn't helping matters.

She bared her teeth at Hilda now. Hilda gasped and took another step backwards. No, Adèle wasn't doing herself any favours at all.

'Adèle . . .' Lorinda advanced a step of her own, blocking Adèle's path and cutting off another circuit of the lamp post. 'Why don't we all go back to my place and have a drink?'

'Oh, no!' Hilda said. 'I mean, thank you, but — But it's so late —'

'I have a better idea.' Adèle's eyes gleamed wickedly. 'Why don't we all get into the car and go for a nice drive?'

'Drive? Now?' Hilda couldn't believe the suggestion had been made. 'Drive where?'

'Oh, just around.' Adèle waved one hand in a descriptive circle. 'No destination — unless we see a likely pub. Just a fun ride.'

'I don't think you'll find a pub still open —' Lorinda began.

'Just ride around? Fun?' It was obvious that Hilda was shocked to the depths of her thrifty soul. 'With no destination? Polluting the atmosphere? Destroying the environment? So wasteful . . . and extravagant.'

'Not really,' Adèle said. 'I think of it as an investment. I do some of my best plotting when I'm riding around aimlessly. It frees my mind to soar.'

'Then you can't be paying proper attention to the road.' Hilda's gaze flicked to the dented bumper again. Not even a sworn affidavit would convince her that the damage had been done before Adèle ever saw the car.

Was she right? When had Adèle actually arrived in the country? Was it possible that she had been here for some time? Driving that car? Perhaps she had intended to visit Dorian earlier? Had she arrived in the village, tired and jetlagged — not paying proper attention, as Hilda had pointed out — accidentally hit the child and driven off in a panic? Later, having had time to reflect and feeling herself safe, she might have thought it less suspicious to revert to her original plan and visit Dorian. Then, having got away with it once, when she saw the opportunity of doing away with her rival . . . Except the result was working against her

— but she could not have anticipated that — or even considered it, if she had acted on the spur of the moment. It was all vague and amorphous, but it would be interesting to get a look at Adèle's passport and see the date stamped for her arrival.

'Oh, look!' Hilda, staring about wildly for an escape route, pointed at the edge of the circle of light from the street lamp. 'Isn't that your cat? What's it doing? Has it seen a mouse?'

'Oh, no!' Lorinda followed the pointing finger to see the little tortoiseshell creeping out of the shadows, inching forward, her determined gaze fixed on her prey: the newly restored teddy bear she had intended for Lorinda.

'Oh, but — but — no!' Lorinda swooped on her delinquent darling. 'No! No! No!' Cuddling the cat in her arms, she explained, 'I'm sorry, but I've got a little pack rat here. She's fixated on those tiny teddy bears. That's why I was here. I was replacing one she'd, er, liberated. But she seems to object.'

'Oh, bless her,' Hilda cooed. 'She wants it back.'

'I know about cats like that.' Adèle viewed But-Known with a colder eye. 'One

260

of my friends has one — and no ring or earring is safe.'

'Exactly. And this shrine isn't safe, either. I'll have to say goodnight now and take her home and secure the cat flap.'

'I'll walk along with you.' Hilda seized her chance eagerly. 'We go in the same direction.'

'Goodnight.' Adèle sketched a sardonic wave in their direction, fully aware of Hilda's relief. 'And sweet dreams!'

Chapter Eighteen

In the morning, But-Known still was not speaking to her. Had-I was also outraged by the locked cat flap. They ate their breakfast with wounded dignity, then retreated to the sofa for another nap. Not even the ring of the telephone disturbed them, although their ears twitched revealingly.

'Lorinda, I have come to a decision,' Gemma announced firmly, quite as though anyone had been disputing her. 'I simply cannot go on this way. I *am* going to consult that hypnotist and Cressie Adair is not going to make a — a Saturnalia out of it!'

'Cressie did get a bit carried away,' Lorinda agreed. 'But in view of, um, everything that's happened, I'm sure she isn't thinking about a big party any more.'

'I should think not! It's quite out of the question! But . . .' Gemma hesitated. 'I . . . I *do* feel I'd like some moral support. Now that Opal is . . . no longer with me.'

'Of course.' Lorinda had the uneasy feeling that she knew what was coming next.

'So, I was hoping . . .' Sure enough, it came. 'A few of my friends. You and Freddie and Macho . . . I suppose Cressie will have to come, too, since she's with Macho and she was so enthusiastic about the idea. Then there'll just be Professor Borley and Betty . . .'

'The usual suspects,' Lorinda murmured, then wished she hadn't.

'Exactly.' Fortunately, it went over Gemma's head. 'I've never done anything remotely like this before and I *do* feel I need the support of my friends.'

'Don't worry, Freddie and I will rally round.' Nothing would keep them away. 'I'm sure Macho and Cressie will, too.' Nothing would keep Cressie away, either, although keeping her out of the action might be harder.

'I'd be so grateful. Now that I've decided, I want to get it over with as soon as possible. Oh, and I wonder if you'd be kind enough to speak to Cressie for me, dear. You know her better than I do and —'

'You want the name of the hypnotist she was planning to call in?'

'Oh, no, dear, I have a perfectly good

one of my own. A charming young man. We did a feature on him in *Woman's Place* shortly before I retired. Everyone was expecting great things of him, but he doesn't seem to have made the breakthrough yet. He's been entertaining on cruise liners, but I understand he's resting this season. I have his number in my contacts book and it's all arranged for tomorrow evening. I hope that isn't too short notice for everyone, but it *is* midweek and quiet.'

'It's fine with me. And everyone else, so far as I know. But what do you want me to talk to Cressie about?'

'Oh, yes. I was just going to ask you if you'd mind passing on the invitation to her. And to Macho. Actually, I rang Macho, but Cressie answered and . . . and I'm afraid I hung up. I don't really feel strong enough — I mean, she's very nice . . . I'm sure . . . and talented . . . but . . .' Gemma trailed off into an awkward silence.

'That's all right,' Lorinda said soothingly. (As though anyone had to produce an excuse for not wanting to talk to Cressie!) 'I'll take care of it.'

'Oh, thank you so much . . .' A flurry of yelps and yaps in the background distracted her. 'I must go now . . . they're . . . Goodbye.'

The cats were genuinely asleep now and Lorinda left the room quietly, although it was probable that nothing would disturb them for a couple of hours.

She ought to ring Cressie, but didn't feel able to cope with that just yet. Despite telling Gemma that Cressie had been thinking twice about her party plans, she was not quite sure that this was the case. It might be safer to wait until the last minute before telling Cressie what was planned. That way, she wouldn't have time to mobilize her media contacts to get down here and turn it into a circus.

That decided, and finding her mind empty of any further ideas for the work in progress, she might as well do something useful and go shopping, rather than sitting in front of a blank screen.

As she left the house by the back door, she thought she saw someone in the upstairs window on the other side of Freddie's semi-detached. She waved cheerily, but Jack or Karla, whichever one it was, appeared not to have seen her. Or wasn't in a friendly mood. The figure moved away and the net curtain fell back into place.

'*Be* like that then,' she muttered and went on her way. Presumably the Jackleys would surface eventually, in their own good time, and decide to rejoin the human race. Meanwhile, best leave them to their own devices. They obviously wanted to be left alone.

The library, the baker, the greengrocer, the butcher, the soothing familiar round restored Lorinda's spirits. Although she still found herself crossing to the other side of the street to avoid walking directly past the shrine. She noticed that she was not the only one to do so. The whole village was finding its presence increasingly unsettling. Oppressive, even. A constant reminder of the unpredictability of life and the sudden tragedy that could engulf people at any moment.

On her return journey, Lorinda noticed a woman standing at the shrine, head bowed and motionless. She was relieved to see that it wasn't Betty Alvin but, as she watched, Betty came along and stopped there. The other woman gave no sign of being aware of her until Betty stepped forward and gently took her arm. The woman tried to turn away, but Betty did not relax her grip and began speaking softly and intently, handing her a tissue. The woman dabbed at her eyes with it and shook her head. Betty continued to insist until, finally, the woman allowed herself to be led away in the direction of the shops.

A nice cup of tea. Lorinda could almost hear Betty saying it. The English panacea — but this was one ill it could not cure, or even help. Obviously, the mourning woman was the child's mother. Equally obviously, she and Betty were old friends. That would explain Betty's interest in the shrine — and her knowledge of the family concerned and the remaining children. It was brave of Betty to attempt to comfort the woman, whose attitude of dejection and desolation was almost too painful to watch.

Gemma was right, Lorinda decided, anything that might help to allay that poor woman's agony was worth trying. Identifying the killer wouldn't bring back the child, but it might bring some surcease to the family. And it might even prevent the killer from killing again.

If he — or she — hadn't already done it again. The spectre of Opal abruptly flitted through her mind. Another accident? Coincidence? There was no shrine to Opal, but she would not be easily forgotten, either. Gemma, too, would feel a lot better if she knew she had done everything possible, however unlikely it might seem.

She had a task of her own, she remembered uneasily. How late could she leave it in the morning to ring Cressie and invite her to Gemma's little soiree? Or perhaps she could wait until afternoon, she did not have the impression that Cressie was an early riser. At least that could be her excuse —

'*Eeeek!*' The shriek was involuntary, as someone gripped her shoulders from behind and swung her around. 'Macho! What do you think you're doing?'

'Escaping!' he wheezed. 'Running away! Getting lost! Sanctuary, my lady, I beg you — sanctuary!'

'Now what?' She did not need to look at the shocked and horrified expression on his face to know where the trouble lay. 'What has Cressie done now?'

'Doing!' he choked. 'Doing! She's doing the sex scenes — a whole stack of them — for the book. And each one is worse than the last! I looked over her shoulder at the screen until I couldn't stand it any more. And I ran — literally ran!'

'I see.' His laboured breath bore witness to the truth of his statement. He looked horrified, overstressed, disbelieving and, possibly, on the verge of a heart attack. 'Take it easy, it can't be that bad.'

'It can — and it is!' He shook his head

and it went on shaking as though it didn't know when to stop. 'I hold no brief for Henry VIII, but even he wouldn't — You don't know! You just don't know!'

'All right, all right,' she soothed, taking his arm and leading him to her house. 'Tell me . . .'

'She has the *Ride of the Valkyries* at full volume on the sound system and she's halfway through a bottle of vodka.' Macho shuddered, accepting a modest gin and tonic. 'She says that's the only way to do it: get blind drunk and write a whole series of sex scenes at the same time — and then slot them into the book whenever the alleged plot can be twisted to accommodate them.'

'I've heard that one before,' Lorinda nodded. It seemed to be a favoured ploy among some romantic novelists. What would their fans think, could they ever see them? Wild-eyed, reeling over their keyboards and well beyond an age when such behaviour could be considered amusing — or even acceptable.

'So have I, but I've never seen it before.' Macho shuddered again. 'It's not a pretty sight. And the things she's writing! I couldn't believe what I was seeing when I read that screen!'

'Strong stuff?' Lorinda could believe it. She could also believe that Macho hadn't read any romantic novels lately. They weren't what they used to be.

'Porn! Absolute porn! And not just soft porn, either!' No, he hadn't read any lately — if, indeed, he ever had. 'I told her I refused to be associated with such filth — even under a pseudonym. That was when she took a great swig of vodka — straight from the bottle — and told me to go and, um, *lose* myself.'

'Never mind . . .' She tried to cheer him without betraying her secret amusement. Poor Macho, a scholar and a gentleman — and the last person on earth who should have got involved with a maneater like Cressie. 'The book will be finished soon and Cressie will move out and back into her old life.'

'Will she?' Macho would not be comforted. 'I wouldn't bet on it. The longer she stays, the less she seems to want to go out, even just around the village. I think she's turning into a recluse.'

'Never!' Lorinda laughed uproariously, she couldn't help it. 'You might become a recluse. Even I might. But not Cressie. She couldn't stay out of the spotlight long enough. She was even planning to hijack poor Gemma's session with a hypnotist — and turn it into a big party with all her media contacts down here to film it, remember?'

'There *is* that. But that was then and this is now. She changes from day to day.' Macho rubbed his forehead, the picture of a man to whom women will for ever be a mystery. 'I don't know . . . I just don't know. I can't keep up with her moods.'

'Or her hangovers, it sounds like. Anyway, that solves one little problem I have. If Cressie is locked in mortal combat with her muse and the vodka bottle, she is definitely unavailable and I can't be blamed for not passing on a message to her.'

'What message?' Macho asked uneasily.

'Gemma is going to have her session with a hypnotist, after all. Tomorrow night. She'd like to have us along for moral support — but she doesn't want Cressie to know until the last possible minute, so that she doesn't have time to round up her contacts and turn it into a media circus.'

'I can't blame her for that.' Macho nodded. 'There shouldn't be any problem. Cressie won't surface until well past noon tomorrow — and she won't be feeling halfway human until late afternoon. I'll tell her we're going over to Gemma's in just enough time for her to spruce herself up. She may be annoyed —'

'I don't really see why she should be. If she's so keen on the idea, there's nothing to stop her holding her own party for her friends later. They can regress without Gemma, that's all.'

'Hmm, yes.' A smile tugged at the corners of Macho's lips. 'Good point. I'll put it to her, if I must. She won't like it, but —'

'But there's a lot you don't like,' Lorinda pointed out. If she and the rest of his friends pointed it out often enough, he might eventually get around to doing something about it.

'There might just be a gleam of hope on the horizon,' Macho admitted. 'At least once or twice, she's muttered something about taking the book to New York herself when it's finished, doing all the publicity and claiming the pseudonym as her own. She's welcome to it — I don't want to be seen to be associated with the whole mess. I'd hate to have anyone think I wrote those ghastly scenes.'

'What about the money?' Lorinda asked sharply. 'She's not going to claim that, too, is she?'

'No problem there,' Macho said. 'The contract has it all safely tied up. She can't get at my share although she probably would, if she could.'

'You're sure?' Neither of them had any illusions about Cressie.

'Positive.' Lorinda hadn't known Macho could smile so nastily. 'If she tries, she's in for a shock. Like the one she'll get tomorrow when she discovers that Gemma is going ahead with her hypnotism privately.'

'I wouldn't say it's very private,' Lorinda demurred. 'A lot of us are going to be there.'

'Compared to what Cressie was planning, it's practically a tête-à-tête.' He gave that smile again, a malevolent glint in his eye. 'No cameras, no hoopla — no reel of film to use for publicity. That's what Cressie had in mind, you know. She thought she could take the film to New York, too, and use it to get publicity. She didn't care whether it was screened here or not. She thought it would be just the sort of thing Americans would lap up.'

'It probably would have been,' Lorinda agreed. 'But why? I mean, it doesn't have anything to do with, um, *Anne Boleyn Is Missing!* Does it?'

'That's not the point. Cressie was going

to act as Mistress of Ceremonies at the Regression Party. The publicity — especially if Gemma was able to provide any clues about the hit-and-run — would have launched her new name in a storm of attention. And, I suspect, she was planning to use it as a demonstration tape to audition for one of those presenter jobs that pay so extravagantly.

'Well . . .' His mouth twisted unpleasantly. 'She's snookered there. And she isn't going to be happy when she finds out.'

Chapter Nineteen

'Lorinda! Freddie!' Gemma swung the door wide. 'How kind of you to come.' She craned her neck to look beyond them. 'Are Macho and Cressie with you?'

'No, haven't seen them all day,' Freddie said.

'They'll be along soon,' Lorinda assured her anxious hostess. Gemma was really in a state. Her hands were fluttering like butterflies. But — wasn't there something missing? 'Where are —'

'I've shut the dogs in the back hall. They were getting so over-excited. And, since I don't know exactly what this entails . . . and they're so protective —'

'It would never do to have them attack the hypnotist,' Freddie agreed gravely.

'Exactly. Come and meet him. He's such a dear boy. It's a shame he hasn't had greater success — but his time will come, I'm sure.' She led them into the living room.

'The clan begins to gather.' Professor Borley rose to greet them. 'What can I get you?' He appeared to have taken permanent charge of Gemma's bar.

Betty Alvin nodded to them warily; there seemed to be something defensive in the way she was clutching her glass. Either she did not entirely approve of the proceedings, or the black-clad young man hovering near her was making her uneasy. He did look rather sinister, all in black relieved only by a glittering pendant on a gold chain around his neck.

The doorbell rang and the young man jumped visibly, his thin wiry body quivering. Highly strung, or possibly suffering a form of stage fright? It must be daunting to step down from the shelter of a proscenium arch into a parlour where one was too closely surrounded by the audience.

'There are the others. Good.' Gemma started for the door. 'As soon as we're all settled with drinks, we can begin.'

The young man quivered again. He did not look happy. Lorinda wondered if Gemma was paying him anything, or had lured him with the promise of future publicity — if she could persuade the current staff of her ex-magazine to agree.

The others returned, Gemma and

Macho still exchanging pleasantries, Cressie following them sullenly. Another one who was not happy at the turn of events and who, if she had really drunk all of that bottle of vodka Macho had seen her with, was probably still hungover.

That didn't stop her from accepting another glass of it, however. She stared resentfully around the room, her gaze finally coming to rest on the young man. That made him quiver, too.

'My dears, allow me to present —' Gemma waved him forward, he moved reluctantly — 'Jeffrey Redmoor, Magician and Hypnotist *Extraordinaire!*'

He sketched a bow and managed to look interested as Gemma reeled off their names before concluding, 'Now then —'

The doorbell rang.

'But . . .' Gemma looked towards the entrance hall, disconcerted. 'But we're all here.'

The doorbell gave another sharp imperious summons.

'I suppose I must . . .' Gemma looked around uncertainly before going to answer it.

'Gemma, my dear, I hope we're not late.' Dorian's voice preceded him into the room. 'You must forgive me, but your mes-

sage on my answering machine was so gar-
bled I had difficulty interpreting it.' He
entered, nodding affably to everyone.

'Oh . . . well . . .' Gemma could barely
speak. His effrontery took her breath away.
'I . . . um . . .' There had been no message
and everyone knew it.

'I made Dorian bring me.' Adèle
Desparta pushed past them. 'I know we're
gate-crashing — and I don't care! As soon
as I heard what was happening here, I had
to come.' She fixed her gaze unerringly on
the unfortunate Jeffrey Redmoor, who was
looking less *extraordinaire* by the moment.

'I insist that you hypnotize me, too! I
have nothing to hide — and I want to
prove it. I can't go on like this!'

'I've tried to tell her.' Dorian shrugged.
'She's confusing hypnotism with a lie de-
tector test.'

'I'll take that, too, if I must. I'll do anything to clear my name!'

'Can you do that?' Cressie's interest was
caught, her eyes gleamed at Jeffrey Redmoor. 'Can you hypnotize more than one
person at a time?'

'Oh, yes. On the cruise ships, I often had
to deal with ten or more volunteers at a
time. They'd mob the stage and wouldn't
let me get away with choosing just one or

two. They all wanted to be in the act.' His eyes were haunted, his quivering had settled down to a steady tremor. Lorinda began to wonder whether he were not so much 'resting' as recovering from a nervous breakdown.

'It isn't advisable, you know. So many.' He gave a reminiscent shudder. 'And when they've been drinking, they all think they're comedians. Sometimes you can't tell whether you've genuinely put them under or not. And that's important, when you come to bring them out of the trance. No, no, one at a time is much better.'

'I'm willing to take my turn,' Adèle said. 'Let's get on with it.'

'Oh, but . . .' Swamped by a stronger personality, Gemma was floundering again. 'I'm not sure . . . That is . . . if Jeffrey doesn't mind . . . ? He only expected me.'

'I'll make it worth your while.' Adèle spoke directly to Jeffrey. He nodded, but did not seem any happier.

'Oh, well . . .' Gemma was also unhappy and nervous. 'What do we do now then? Sit in a circle and hold hands?'

'Not unless you want the victims to join us.' Dorian did not bother to conceal his amusement. 'That's the drill for a séance.'

'Oh, well, *I* don't know . . .' Flustered, Gemma looked around helplessly. 'I thought . . . I mean, I'd heard something about circles . . .'

'Just sit down and make yourself comfortable.' Jeffrey Redmoor spoke with sudden authority, assuming his professional persona. 'All of you.'

There was a general shuffling about for chairs. Macho and Cressie bagged the ones nearest to the armchair Jeffrey was settling Gemma into. Adèle pulled a chair closer on the other side. They didn't intend to miss anything.

'Anyone for a refill before this starts?' Professor Borley was remaining by the bar. No one bothered to answer him. Suddenly, the occasion had gone beyond the social.

In the expectant silence, tension eddied through the room and into the farthest corners of the flat. Even the dogs seemed to sense it. Muffled yelps sounded on the far side of the door leading from the kitchen into the back hall.

Jeffrey Redmoor leaned over Gemma and began speaking softly. Macho and Adèle leaned forward, so did Cressie.

Betty Alvin watched intently as Redmoor removed the chain and pendant from around his neck. He swung the pendant slowly in front of Gemma's face. Her eyes followed it.

Lorinda blinked and looked away to find Freddie also blinking. They grimaced slightly at each other and settled farther back in their chairs, distancing themselves.

Dorian got up and sauntered over to join Professor Borley at the bar. He stood there observing the scene as though it were a private performance being staged for his own personal entertainment and casually refilled his glass.

'Oh!' The clink of glass against bottle distracted Gemma, her eyes, which had been closing, flew open. 'Oh, *do* help yourselves. I forgot to tell you. I'm sorry . . .'

'It's all right.' Redmoor gently cradled her cheek with one hand, turning her face away from the others and back to him. 'You're doing fine.' It would take more than Dorian wandering around the room to unsettle him, he had encountered far worse with the drunken revellers on the cruise ships.

'Just let yourself relax . . . it's all right to feel sleepy . . .' He droned on, voice deliberately soothing and expressionless.

'Yes . . . yes. I'm sorry . . . I'll pay attention . . .'

'You don't need to pay attention. You

need to relax . . . you're so tired. Take a deep breath . . . and another . . . and yawn. Think how nice it would be to fall asleep right now . . . no one would mind. You're among friends . . .'

'Yes . . . friends.' Gemma yawned. 'Oh, I'm so sorry!'

'No need to apologize . . . no one minds. You can yawn all you like . . .'

Gemma yawned again. Macho yawned, too. Lorinda tightened her own jaw muscles in an effort to resist the contagion. Even Freddie succumbed, although with another rueful grimace.

After that, everything seemed to go on for an inordinate length of time. Time enough for Dorian to snag another drink, and for Professor Borley to tiptoe lumberously amongst them, refreshing their own drinks. Time enough for boredom to begin to set in. She had to resist a strong temptation to turn to Freddie and start a conversation.

When Redmoor finally straightened up, she would not have been surprised had he admitted defeat and called for a drink. Instead, he gave a faint nod of satisfaction, as at a job well done.

'Now we can begin,' he said.

'Aren't you going to stick a pin in her

first?' Cressie demanded, watching Gemma's blank face avidly.

'Why would I want to do that?' Redmoor looked at her with distaste.

'To make sure she's really in a trance, of course.' The look Cressie gave him doubted his ability, his credentials and perhaps even his antecedents.

'I can assure you she is.' He gave Cressie a *Heaven deliver me from amateurs* look and turned away, dismissing her. He bent over Gemma again, murmuring softly.

'Now . . . you are back there . . . in that time you must remember . . .' He raised his voice to encompass his audience. 'Open your eyes and tell me what you see.'

'Conqueror — no!' Gemma shrieked, her eyes wide open and staring into space. 'Lionheart — stop! Bad dogs! Bad dogs! Stop!'

In the distance, the pugs began barking wildly, hurling themselves against the closed door.

'No . . . no . . .' Redmoor slid a hand across Gemma's forehead and eyes. 'Go back to sleep. It's all right . . . all right . . .'

Gemma's eyes closed, her breathing quietened.

'Sorry,' he apologized, turning to the others. 'I haven't tried this sort of regression before. One can never be sure how the subject will react.'

'A little less emotion is called for, I think,' Professor Borley suggested helpfully.

'Yes, yes, that's right.' The nervous quiver had returned. Redmoor no longer seemed so completely in control of the situation, but he turned back to Gemma.

'You are calm . . . you are tranquil . . .' he intoned. 'It is all in the past. You are looking back from a great distance. You can see it all . . . but it no longer upsets you. You are above it all . . . you can talk about it. You are there . . . but not physically. Now . . . open your eyes again . . . Look around . . . and tell us what you were seeing on that unhappy night . . . what you were thinking . . .'

'Unhappy, yes . . .' Gemma sighed, but was otherwise calm. 'So dark and rainy . . . cold . . . What is that child doing out so late on a night like this? No, Conqueror, we're not going that way tonight . . . We want to get back —'

'I don't like these people.' Another voice cut across hers. 'I don't like the look of them. What are we doing in this place? Is this what you meant by "a bit of rough"?'

'Great Lord! He's overshot his mark!'

284

Dorian began to laugh into the stunned silence. 'The idiot has put Macho under, too!'

'Let's think of some good questions to ask!' Freddie snorted. Betty Alvin giggled nervously.

'Quiet, please, quiet!' Redmoor pleaded desperately. 'You mustn't startle them . . . wake them at this stage. It might be dangerous.'

'Why did he go under and not me?' Adèle was aggrieved. 'I was the one who *wanted* to be hypnotized!'

'Please . . . please . . .'

'As an informed guess, I'd say Macho is a lot more suggestible than you are.' Dorian was still chuckling.

'Please . . . this is not a joke. The consequences to them could be serious.'

'There's a car coming along behind us,' Gemma said. 'I can hear it, but not see it. Its headlights are too dim. And it doesn't sound roadworthy. All those rattling noises. I'm sure it's not safe . . .'

A rattly car, barely roadworthy. Lorinda could not resist a sideways glance at Betty Alvin, who seemed no longer disposed to giggle.

'Don't think I don't recognize that smell in the air . . .' Macho sounded cross, he

285

spoke with more animation than Gemma. Perhaps that instruction about calm had been so directed at her that it had by-passed him. 'I used to be a schoolteacher, you know. It's not unknown to me. Is that why you've brought us here? To pick up a fresh supply of whatever drug you use?'

'Shut up, you fool!' Cressie snapped.

'Doggies, doggies, why are you so rest-less tonight? The sooner I get you home the better. I don't know what's got into you both tonight.'

'That man over there, the one who looks like a bouncer.' Macho lifted his head and looked into the distance. 'I think he's waving at you. Do you know him?'

'Shut up! Shut up!' Cressie lurched for-ward, hand raised to strike. Adèle caught her arm and pushed her back into her seat.

'He may be suggestible, but he doesn't like orders,' Abby Borley observed. 'I can't say I blame him.'

'Silence! I insist!' Redmoor had found his authority again. 'If not, I clear the room! All of you — out!'

That startled them into the silence he required.

'You can't —' Cressie began.

'I can — and I will! The safety of my subjects is of paramount importance! I will not have it endangered!'

'He's right,' Abby Borley said. 'I think we'd better do as he says. He's the man who knows.'

'Leave? Now? But we've just arrived,' Macho protested. 'Oh . . . is it because that man in the corner is shaking his fist at you? He seems to know you . . . he doesn't seem to like you.'

'Shut your mouth, damn you!' Cressie snarled. She made another lunge towards him, but Adèle was ready. Cressie found herself hurled back into her seat. Adèle moved forward and stood over her, blocking any further moves.

'No, Lionheart, no!' Gemma said. 'You've investigated that lamp post quite long enough. Now do what you must and hurry up about it. I want to get home and — *Oh!* Oh, no! No . . .'

'No!' Macho said. 'No! What's going on here? He's coming this way — the bouncer and another yob are with him. Are those guns? No . . . perhaps not . . . they seem to be pipes and a crowbar. Heavy, like bludgeons . . . they're going to —'

'Pipes . . .' Gemma said. 'Those are pipes sticking out of the back of the white van. That's what's doing the rattling — most of it. And that ladder on the roof . . .

but I still think — Oh! It's skidding!'

'Run!' Macho said. 'Run! Yes — run! *Beat our brains out!* That's what they're shouting. They mean it. Why?'

Cressie opened her mouth, Adèle put her hand over it.

'Fine . . .' Redmoor encouraged impartially. 'You're doing just fine. Keep on. Everything you could see . . . everything you were thinking . . .'

The doorbell pealed sharply through the room. Everyone jumped. Redmoor cursed softly, bending anxiously over his subjects.

'I'll get it!' Betty scampered to answer the door before the bell rang again.

'Are they all right?' Abby Borley asked.

'I think so.' Redmoor straightened up, frowning towards the door. 'Don't let —'

'They're gaining on us!' Macho was becoming agitated. 'Hurry! Hurry!'

'Those brakes! They're not holding! Conqueror! Lionheart! Stop it! No! No! You're pulling me over!' Gemma, too, was losing her tranquil perspective. '*Eeeek! Ooooh!* . . . My ankle . . . my ankle . . . the pain . . .' She began to cry.

'A taxi!' Macho shouted. 'Grab it! Grab it! We've got to get away!'

'I'll bring them out of it.' Redmoor was

perspiring. 'There's no use trying to go on now.'

'*Hey!*' Jack and Karla Jackley burst into the room ahead of Betty. 'The prodigals return — and there's a party waiting! How about that!'

'Great timing!' Freddie viewed them with disfavour. 'Couldn't you have sulked in your tent a while longer?'

'Huh? Whadda you mean?' Jack looked around the room: no one appeared happy to see them. 'Are we interrupting something?'

Gemma's sobs died away, Macho shook his head, both seemed dazed and bewildered.

'Are they going to be all right?' Adèle asked. 'They look . . . You know, I've changed my mind. I don't think I want to be next, after all.'

'What do you mean — sulking?' Jack was still mulling over his unenthusiastic reception. 'What are you talking about? What tent?'

'I'm sorry if we're intruding,' Karla apologized. 'We didn't realize. We were so excited about getting home. We were just this minute driving up and we saw the cats sitting in the window box looking in the window. So we knew you must be in here and we thought we'd stop here first and say, "Hello, we're back." '

'Back? This minute? Stop here first?' Freddie echoed, staring at them. 'You mean you've just got back? You haven't been home already for days and days?'

'Of course not.' Karla frowned. 'You'd have seen us long ago if we had.'

'And you haven't rented your house out? Or loaned it to friends?'

'Hell no!' Jack said. 'What would we do a thing like that for, when there was no telling how long we'd be away?'

'Then . . .' Freddie asked, 'who's been living in your side of the house?'

Chapter Twenty

'You mean there are squatters?' Dorian's eyebrows rose. 'In Brimful Coffers?'

'In our house?' Karla's concern was more personal. 'Someone is trying to steal our house out from under us? Just because we don't happen to be there for a while?'

'That's what squatting is.' Dorian shrugged.

'That's stupid!' Jack said. 'Anyway, it won't do them any good. The house doesn't belong to us, we're only renting.'

'I'm not sure that actually makes any difference,' Dorian said. 'Possession being eleven points of the law and all that.'

'Eleven?' Jack said. 'But —'

'That's what happens when you quote too accurately,' Professor Borley noted. 'No one believes it, the original has been misquoted so often.'

'I don't believe they intend to keep the house.' Freddie was following another train of thought. 'I think they just want to borrow it for a while.'

'Borrow our house?' Karla was unbelieving. 'Why? Who?'

'Hilda Saint was telling me . . .' Lorinda was reminded. 'Her builders were getting to work in better time . . . now that they had found a place to stay locally.'

'Builders would know how to get into a locked-up house.' Freddie nodded. 'And they're never too careful about other people's property. That would explain some of the thumps and crashes I've been hearing.'

'Thumps? Crashes?' Karla froze. 'If they've broken any of my antiques —'

'Why would builders want to move into our house?' Jack couldn't understand it. 'Is it some kind of scam? Do they make all kinds of repairs and changes and then send us a dirty great bill and expect us to pay it? Is that their game?'

'An interesting question, but I think there's a simpler answer.' Macho had been listening intently. 'Would you like to provide it, Cressie?'

'Me? Why me?' Cressie was all wide-eyed innocence. 'What have I got to do with it?'

'Come off it,' Freddie snorted. 'It's our business to figure out clues. After what we've heard tonight, do you think we can't put your little two and two together?'

'That's right,' Adèle agreed. 'And I was there when Hilda said she'd read *Mooning the Builders* and it was so similar to what she was experiencing it was like déjà vu. She thought it was because builders were all alike. But they're the same builders, aren't they, Cressie?'

'How would I know? I've never seen —'

'Added to which, I can remember everything I saw while in my trance,' Macho warned. 'And more seems to be coming back to me now. Our taxi was followed for quite a while, Cressie. . . . I can remember you kept looking out the back window and urging the driver to hurry . . . and to take all sorts of sudden turnings . . .'

'You're lying!' Cressie gasped. 'You couldn't remember anything. You were out cold!'

'We lost them finally — and you were limp with relief. But they must have noted the area where we disappeared and come back searching for you. Why do they hate you so much?'

'They . . . they didn't like the book about them . . .'

'Neither did a lot of the critics, but they're not trying to beat your brains out.'

'Well . . . maybe the cheque bounced . . . I lose track sometimes of how much I have in my account. And anyway, they hadn't done the work — not properly. They were trying to cheat me.'

And possibly, Lorinda thought, there was a personal element involved, as Hilda Saint had suggested. When Cressie ended an affair, it was unlikely to be with any tact or delicacy — especially when finances were involved. And there was something else Hilda had said . . .

'Those threatening notes pushed under your door in the middle of the night . . .' She turned to Gemma. 'Are you sure Adèle wrote them to Opal?'

'Threatening notes? To Opal?' Adèle was indignant. 'I wouldn't lower myself! And I'd certainly never push them under doors in the middle of the night.'

'And you're not the sort to let doors slam behind you at that hour, either,' Freddie said. 'That's the sort of thing builders are noted for.'

'Gemma, what makes you think they were threatening Opal — and not you?' Lorinda asked.

'Why should anyone want to threaten me?' Gemma was incredulous. 'What did I ever do to anyone? Apart from a few rejection slips, that is. You don't suppose . . .'

'What, actually, did those notes say?'

'Oh, I don't know . . . they were awfully vague . . . "Keep out" . . . "Mind your own business" . . . Opal tore them up — she said it was the best way to handle it. I thought she knew what she was doing . . . I thought they were meant for her. They *must* have been. Who'd threaten me?'

'Everyone in the village knew you were talking about going to a hypnotist,' Freddie said. 'Someone must have been afraid of what you might retrieve from your memory. It might not be admissible evidence in court, but it might be enough to start the police looking in the right direction for proof.'

'Oh, but it didn't work, did it? I mean, I don't feel as though anything happened. Anything useful . . .'

'Don't you remember what you said?' Cressie asked.

'Well . . . in a way . . . it seems part of a dream . . .' Gemma was becoming agitated.

'Never mind,' Freddie said. 'We all heard you and we can testify, if necessary.'

Betty Alvin coughed softly and they looked towards her, waiting to hear what she might add.

'Yes, Betty?' Dorian gave her an encouraging smile. 'What is it?'

'No, nothing.' Embarrassed, she shook her head. 'I wasn't going to say anything. I just —' She coughed again.

'Wait a minute.' Adèle lifted her head and sniffed. 'Does anyone smell smoke?'

They could all smell it now — and see it. A dark curl of smoke drifted along the ceiling from the direction of the kitchen.

'She's left something to burn in the oven,' Dorian said. 'Typical!'

'No!' Abruptly, Gemma was on her feet and rushing towards the kitchen. 'I haven't used the oven in days.'

'Calm, please be calm. You should sit quietly for a bit,' Redmoor protested. 'And so should you,' he added, as Macho followed her along with the others.

'You see?' Gemma turned to Dorian triumphantly. 'There's nothing on fire here!'

'No,' Dorian agreed. 'The smoke seems to be coming from your back hall.'

'The hall? The dogs are out there! Conqueror! Lionheart!' she called.

There was an ominous silence. Lorinda realized that they had not heard the pugs barking for some time.

'Lionheart! Conqueror! Doggies — answer me!' With rising panic, Gemma hurled herself at the door and struggled with it. 'I can't — I can't open the door.'

'You're probably a little weak after your trance.' Professor Borley stepped forward. 'Let me try.' He began confidently, but his face turned puce as the door resisted his efforts.

'Smoke inhalation!' Gemma wailed. 'They're overcome . . . lying there . . . still inhaling all that smoke . . .'

The smoke *was* getting thicker.

'Can I have a little back-up here?' Borley called over his shoulder.

Macho, Jack and Redmoor rushed to help him.

'Sorry.' Dorian held back and shrugged to Adèle's accusing eyes. 'I'm still recovering from my last war wounds.'

'It must be locked,' Redmoor said. 'Where's the key?'

'Knowing Gemma, it's on the other side,' Dorian said.

'No,' Gemma began. 'No —'

'Right. All together now,' Borley ordered. 'One . . . two . . . three!' They hit the door. The lock splintered, but the door held.

'It must be blocked in some way.' Macho rubbed his shoulder. 'I suggest we —'

'I suggest we call the fire brigade and get out of here,' Adèle said. 'Not necessarily in that order.'

'I've just tried to call the fire brigade.' White-faced, Betty appeared in the doorway behind them. 'There was no dial tone. The line is dead.'

'Nonsense!' Gemma said. 'I was talking to Hilda Saint just an hour ago. It was all right then. I told her —'

'This door is getting pretty hot around the edges,' Jack interrupted. 'I don't think we should stick around here.'

'Oh, but —' Only Gemma was prepared to argue.

'Once outside, we can go around the side of the building and get at the hall that way.' Abby Borley put his arm around her shoulders and led her firmly to the front door.

Cressie was already there, fighting to open the door. It looked like a losing battle.

'I can't move it,' she said. 'It won't budge. I can't even turn the knob.'

'I'll get it,' Jack pushed her aside. 'Sometimes it takes brute force.' He tried that, then moved aside as Redmoor advanced. 'Okay, see what you can do.'

'It's no good. It's stuck or . . .' Redmoor looked around at them. 'It feels as though there's some sort of wedge under the doorknob.'

'At least the window will open.' Dorian had been experimenting. 'It may be undignified, but it looks as though we'll have to go out that way.'

There was a sudden outburst of hysterical barks as Dorian slid the window up as high as it would go and pulled the curtains aside.

'The dogs!' Gemma gasped. 'They're out there! Oh, thank heavens. They're safe!'

'Which is more than can be said for us,' Freddie pointed out grimly.

'What . . . do you mean?' No, Gemma wasn't gasping, she was wheezing.

'She means — who let them out?' Adèle translated, with equal grimness.

'Also — who blocked the front and back doors, leaving us only one way out?' Freddie was relentless. 'A way we'll have to take one at a time.'

'And who's waiting outside to pick us off —' Macho began to cough.

'As we climb out one by one?' Lorinda finished for him.

'We can't stay here.' Tears were beginning to roll down Betty's face, although not from emotion. 'Those fumes are noxious.'

'They can't be!' Gemma protested.

'There's nothing out there but my shopping basket and a couple of pairs of wellington boots. They might smell but —'
She broke off, coughing.

'Nice playmates you have, Cressie.' Freddie gave her a cold look. 'They came prepared to kill us — one way or another.'

'Never mind the recriminations,' Adèle said. 'We've got to get out of here.'

'Quite right,' Freddie agreed. 'Who wants to go first? Don't all rush at once,' she added, as most of them took an involuntary step backwards.

'Look.' Only Jack stood his ground. 'This is stupid! We can't just stay here and fry!'

'Roast, I think,' Freddie corrected.

' "With one bound, Jack was free,", eh?' Dorian raised a sardonic eyebrow. 'Go ahead. I've always wanted to see how that one worked.'

'Jack's right,' Karla said. 'Let's rush them! There's got to be more of us than there are of them.'

'Ah, Americans! So impetuous!' Dorian said. 'Unfortunately, all ten of us can't crowd through one window at the same time. That rather puts a damper on your idea.'

'There are three of them,' Macho said.

'Aren't there, Cressie?'

'I . . . I don't know . . . probably,' she admitted.

'We've got to do something!' Karla looked around wildly.

'Let me make a constructive suggestion,' Dorian proposed. 'Since our friends seem to want Cressie so much, why don't we let her be first through the window?'

'Dorian!' Adèle was shocked. She obviously didn't know Dorian as well as the others did. 'You can't mean that!'

'It might work,' Jack said. 'I mean, she could keep them busy for a minute while the rest of us get out — and then we can rescue her.'

'Oh, yes?' Cressie was not the stuff of which sacrificial lambs were made. 'And how do I keep them from killing me meanwhile?'

'You could always write them another cheque,' Macho snarled. 'They might let you live until they find out whether it bounces.'

'The situation has gone beyond Cressie,' Freddie reminded them. 'The one they really want now is Gemma. She's the one who can testify against them. They've already tried for her once.'

'They have? You mean —' Gemma didn't

want to believe it. 'Opal . . . ?'

'It was a dark rainy night, you're both about the same size and there's the family resemblance. The dogs clinched it. They saw them and thought they had you.'

'And I sent her out with them!' Gemma wailed.

'That's it!' Adèle was relieved. 'And just because Opal and I were rivals, everyone blamed me. Now they'll have to —'

There was a sudden outburst of shrill barks and yelps.

'The dogs!' Gemma cried. 'They'll save us!' She dashed to the window and called loudly: 'Conqueror — Lionheart — *Sic them!* Attack! Attack!'

There were hoots of derisive laughter in the distance.

'I'm afraid they've got the measure of your mutts, Gemma,' Dorian said.

'What the hell!' Jack started forward. 'Things can't get any worse!'

'*Prrryeeeow* . . .' Roscoe sailed through the open window, Had-I and But-Known following.

'No!' 'Oh, no!' With cries of consternation, Macho and Lorinda stooped to gather up their darlings.

'You had to open your big mouth!' Karla told Jack.

302

'Here . . .' They had discreetly ignored it when Professor Borley slipped into the bathroom. Now he was back, his arms loaded with wet towels. 'Wrap these around your heads, they'll filter the smoke — and they might give some protection when we try the window.'

'Good thinking!' Jack reached eagerly for a dripping bath towel.

'Can't we wring it out a bit first?' Karla complained, holding hers at arm's length.

'Not on my carpet!' Gemma winced.

'Carpets are the least of our problems!' Abby Borley was losing patience. 'Now — while I was looking around in there, I noticed the bathroom has a transom window opening on to Coffers Passage. It's too small and too high for our builders to bother worrying about. But —' He turned to Redmoor — 'you're small enough, young enough and, I hope, agile enough to be able to get through it. If you're willing to try, that is?'

'Is there a choice?' Redmoor was already striding towards the bathroom, wrapping a navy blue towel around his head.

'Don't all follow,' Dorian warned. 'They can see in from outside and they'll get suspicious if the room empties.'

'We ought to turn off the lights,' Macho

said. 'We won't be so visible then.'

'I'm sorry —' Gemma gave a little whimper. 'I don't think I could bear the darkness.' Lorinda was glad that Gemma made the protest; none of them really wanted to be left in darkness.

'We'll turn off most of the lights then,' Macho compromised, and did so, leaving only one lamp in the far corner still glowing.

'He made it on the second try,' Borley reported, returning. 'So far, no one seems to have spotted him.'

'They wouldn't know him anyway, he's never been in town before,' Dorian said. 'Gemma is just a one-night stand for him, so to speak.' No one reacted, not even Gemma.

'So now we just have to stay here and wait?' There was a ragged edge to Cressie's voice.

'Unless you have a better idea,' Freddie said.

'I think we've seen enough of Cressie's ideas,' Dorian said. 'If it weren't for her, we wouldn't be in this mess!'

Not quite. If Macho hadn't brought her here . . . Lorinda and Freddie exchanged glances, trying not to look at Macho — or Cressie.

'Don't worry!' Cressie snapped. 'I've had enough of all of you! As soon as we get out of here — *if* we get out of here — I'm going straight back to London!'

'I'll be able to leave, too,' Adèle said. 'And no one will be able to accuse me of running away.'

Dorian could not conceal a brief smile of satisfaction.

'I'll be glad to see the last of this dump!' Cressie was not finished. 'And you —' She glared at Macho. 'You can go back to sleep — or whatever you do — with your tame harem!'

'Harem?' It was not until Freddie spluttered with sudden hysterical laughter that Lorinda realized Cressie meant them.

'Harem?' Macho looked at them both and a slow smile began to spread across his face.

'It's not *that* funny!' Lorinda snapped.

'No,' Macho agreed, but he was still smiling. 'Perhaps it's not.'

'Listen.' Professor Borley called them back to order, one hand upraised in the call for silence.

The others stood frozen abruptly in listening attitudes. It had suddenly gone unnaturally quiet outside.

'Do you think they've gone away?'

Gemma quavered hopefully.

'Don't bet on it.' Jack was prowling by the open window. 'I think there's somebody moving around out there . . . trying to sneak up on us . . . What the —'

An unidentifiable object flew through the open window. Jack caught it and threw it back. There was a crash as the object shattered on the pavement outside and burst into flames.

'Jeez!' Jack said. 'That was a Molotov cocktail!'

'Do they have any more?' Karla wanted to know.

'We're gonna find out, I'm afraid.' Jack flexed his muscles. 'Get me something I can bat them with —'

'WHAT DO YOU THINK YOU'RE DOING?'

The sudden indignant bellow spoiled the thrower's aim.

The next missile hit the outer frame of the window and sent a river of fire down the side.

'WHERE HAVE YOU BEEN ALL DAY? I'm not paying you to go out and moonlight on someone else's building site all day and then play with fireworks all night!'

'It's Hilda,' Gemma said. 'I was going to

tell you I invited her to drop over for a drink later. I thought we'd be finished by about now . . .'

'We almost were,' Freddie muttered.

'COME BACK WHEN I'M TALKING TO YOU! What's going on here? If you think —'

A siren sounded in the distance, approaching rapidly.

'Jeffrey has made it!' Gemma exulted. 'The dear boy has brought help! I hope it's the fire brigade . . . although the police . . .'

'At this point, I'd welcome the Boy Scouts,' Dorian said. 'We're in no position to be choosy.'

'Cressie was true to her word,' Macho said, a trifle smugly. 'I understand she barely paused in London long enough to pack and she must be in New York by now. With any luck, she'll stay there.'

'Don't you think she'll come back for the trial?' Lorinda pondered. The police in the next county had caught the fleeing builders, initially for speeding, compounded by resisting arrest and driving an unroadworthy vehicle while banned from driving at all. There had been plenty to hold them on before the additional charges of homicide, arson and attempted murder came through.

'Not if she can help it,' Macho said. 'They won't bother about her, her evidence isn't necessary. Gemma is the main witness.'

'It's so nice of Professor Borley to take both Gemma and Betty to Cornwall for a fortnight's holiday,' Lorinda said. 'They were badly in need of it — and I don't think they could have afforded it by themselves.'

'I wonder who's chaperoning whom in that little trio?' Freddie mused.

'All the same, it's not a bad idea.' Macho looked from one to the other. 'You know, my bank balance is in a pretty healthy state at the moment — even if it is thanks to Cressie. Why don't I treat the three of us to a little holiday of our own? Perhaps Spain, or Italy, or one of those cruises Dorian is always going on about?'

There was a long considering silence, broken only by the purring of the three cats, each settled comfortably on a lap.

'Just the three of us,' Freddie teased. 'You and your harem?'

'That's what they'll be saying, won't they?' Lorinda said thoughtfully. 'After the way Cressie accused us —'

'Borley and *his* harem are in no position to talk,' Macho said. 'And, as for Dorian —'

'Do we care?' Freddie grinned conspiratorially at them both. 'Let them talk. Everything will sort itself out eventually.'

'That's right.' Macho stretched, disturbing a Roscoe who had gone from gaunt to sleek and was now on his way back to plump. Roscoe complained briefly, then settled down again, leading the chorus of purrs from Had-I and But-Known, his own harem — such as it was.

'We've got our own peaceful life back again.' Macho spoke for everyone. 'And that's all I care about.'

About the Author

Marian Babson was born in Salem, Massachusetts, but has lived in London for the greater part of her life. She has worked as a librarian, managed a campaign headquarters, been a receptionist, secretary and den mother to a firm of commercial artists and was co-editor of a knitting-machine magazine, despite the fact she can't knit, even with two needles. A long sojourn as a temp sent her into the heart of business life all over London, working for architects, law firms, the British Museum, a Soho Club and even a visiting superstar. She also served as secretary to the Crime Writers' Association.

Marian Babson is now a full-time writer and her many interests including theatre, cinema, art, cooking, travel and cats, are reflected in her books.

We hope you have enjoyed this Large Print book. Other Thorndike, Wheeler or Chivers Press Large Print books are available at your library or directly from the publishers.

For more information about current and upcoming titles, please call or write, without obligation, to:

Publisher
Thorndike Press
295 Kennedy Memorial Drive
Waterville, ME   04901
Tel. (800) 223-1244

Or visit our Web site at:
www.gale.com/thorndike
www.gale.com/wheeler

OR

Chivers Large Print
published by BBC Audiobooks Ltd
St James House, The Square
Lower Bristol Road
Bath BA2 3SB
England
Tel. +44(0) 800 136919
email: bbcaudiobooks@bbc.co.uk
www.bbcaudiobooks.co.uk

All our Large Print titles are designed for easy reading, and all our books are made to last.